Vlad V (Book 5)
The Queen of Vampires

A New Queen Arises

By **Mit Sandru**

Artwork by Dumitru Sandru

Chivileri Publishing

ISBN 13: 978-1-942612-07-0

Disclaimer:

This is a fictional story. All names, persons, organizations, businesses, occurrences, and places, except for historical locations, are fictitious and arise solely from the imagination of the author. Any resemblances to actual people or events are completely coincidental.

Table of Contents

The previous book in this series is Vampires of Transylvania (Vlad V Book 4)

Pray that you won't become their prey.

Cat Sanders has a simple task: spread Vlad V Draculesti's ashes in Transylvania at midnight, during full moon. But it won't be that simple. Vlad V, and Vlad the Impaler's old vampire enemies abduct her and her Romanian friend, Dr. Tudor Lupu. While in captivity they discover the Vampire Queen's proto-vampire and zombie army, which are held in hibernation to be used for mayhem and destruction whenever the queen so wishes. She and Dr. Tudor might not be allowed to see the light of day again. Cat's only hope for rescue is her vampire friend, Mundibuto, who is presently in Transylvania. Will they be able to escape from the blood sucking proto-vampires, and flesh-eating zombies, or become zombies themselves?

Chapter 1. Cat

The Bran Castle in Transylvania seemed to howl: *This Belongs to Dracula!* With tall, crenelated white walls and orange clay tile roofs, it stands high on the hill, towering over the valley and the roads below. Dr. Tudor Lupu and I—Cat Sanders, the great-great-granddaughter of the vampire Vlad V Draculesti—were touring this famous castle, trying to recover from the ordeal we had undergone in Sighisoara only a week before. Now, holding hands, we were just two tourists who were, perhaps, in love. In a very short period of time, I had grown fond of my new Romanian friend.

"Wow!" I couldn't help expressing my surprise at the old castle. I looked down into the inner courtyard, with its limited sunshine even at high noon and a well in its center, it seemed to be a castle where the sleeping beauty might still be lying in one of the higher towers.

"Impressive, isn't it, Cat?" said Tudor, my doctor beau and lover, gesturing at the balconies and open corridors crisscrossing the inner courtyard walls, leading to the interior chambers. We visited some of the chambers with their cozy fireplaces, low ceilings, and small lead-glass windows. There were secret passages, some known and others still unknown, that gave a foreboding impression.

"A castle worthy of Dracula," I said.

"Yes, it is, except this wasn't Dracula's castle," said Tudor. "It was originally built by the Teutonic Knights and then rebuilt from stone as a fortress in the 14th century by the German Saxons. In early 20th century, it became the property of the Romanian royal family, and Queen Marie used it as her personal castle. After the communists took over Romania, it was nationalized. And after they fell from power, the castle was given back to the descendants of the royal family. It is privately owned now, but it's still a museum."

In spite of its notoriety, I didn't find any mentions of this castle in my great- grandfather's records. Dracula, Vlad the Impaler, and his nephew Vlad V apparently never lived in this castle, although they may have traveled the nearby roads centuries ago.

"It is for sale." Tudor winked at me. "Why don't you buy it, Cat?"

I looked into his green eyes to see if he was joking. He was half-serious. "What would I do with a castle-museum?"

He shrugged. "Redecorate it." He took me by the hand into another low-ceilinged chamber that was furnished with dark wooden benches and cupboards. It felt cozy in there. I kissed him, and he gently caressed the back of my neck. Damn, I still got goose bumps when we kissed.

A group of tourists entered the room, so we had to interrupt our pleasant interlude, and we continued our tour of the medieval castle. As we walked around, I kept a cautious eye out for any signs of vampires.

It had been one week since our deadly encounter with Queen Eleonore's army of proto-vampires and zombies, and with, of course, her three killer vampires: Ilie, Nicolae, and Fakeula. We survived that confrontation. We killed the vampires and destroyed her army with lots of help from Mundibuto, my vampire friend, and the Strigoi, my ghostly bodyguards. Tudor took me to a spa with hot and cold springs and therapeutic mud baths to relax and soothe our fried nerves. I hadn't had any negative psychological backlash from the horrible encounter, as I had experience with vampires and their deadly attacks, but I wasn't so sure about Tudor, who thought vampires were the stuff of legends. Now he knew better. Modern vampires know how to keep a low profile, even in Transylvania.

Of course, the vampires most people are familiar with are from stories, like those popularized by Bram Stoker in his book *Dracula*. Real vampires are completely different from the bloodsucking, murdering, and undead vampires of yore. Real vampires are not dead, and they have blue blood. They live among us, the sun doesn't burn them, and they're not afraid of crosses or garlic. And you can see them in a mirror. They don't kill their victims, and once bitten, the victims don't become vampires. It is true that real vampires drink human blood, but not for nourishment; it serves them as a life elixir. That's what keeps them alive for so long without aging. Their nourishment is alcohol. They don't eat food like humans do. Instead, they consume copious amounts of booze without ever getting drunk. I suppose their vampire livers—if they even have livers—can handle the alcohol, and their metabolism converts the alcohol into energy.

Tudor was holding up pretty well, considering the mayhem we had experienced in the crypt under the cemetery on Sighisoara's hill. I kept a loving eye on him and a vigilant eye on everyone around us. I didn't think we were in much danger from Queen Eleonore's other vampires, especially since Mundibuto was hunting for her and her subjects. Most likely she was in hiding, fearing the wrath of Mundibuto.

But I had to be alert to what could happen while I was still in Transylvania. So why was I lingering here? Returning to New York would not have appeased the queen's fury. If they want to get you, vampires don't care about borders or secure enclaves. And unless Mundibuto could convince the queen to stand down and not come after me, vigilance—not hiding—was prudent for now.

As we walked in an outdoor corridor of the inner courtyard, I spotted, on a balcony on the opposite side, two vampires I hadn't expected to see here, and so soon.

Chapter 2. Cat

With big smiles on their faces, François and Angelique—my vampire friends—stood with their arms crossed, staring through their large dark sunglasses at us. Both of them were dressed in beige and khaki-colored clothes with long sleeves to hide their paleness. François's black hair was silver-blond now, and Angelique's red hair was tinted black. They had taken precautions and changed their appearances to prevent Interpol from recognizing them. They were wanted internationally.

Last I knew, François was back in New York City taking care of Angelique, who was recovering from the white-fog drug and the bullets she'd received while battling the nasty Silver Coffin cult. What could have brought them here? Probably Queen Eleonore von Schwarzenberg problem.

François made a slight gesture with his head to meet them inside a castle room to our right. I nodded in acknowledgment.

"Come this way, Tudor." I took him by the hand and pulled him after me.

"We've seen that part already," he said, unaware of my quiet exchange with François.

I turned and placed a hand on the side of his face. "I need to meet some other vampire friends of mine. Come."

With his eyebrows raised, he followed me while holding my hand. "Mundibuto? I didn't see him."

I shook my head.

"Who, then?" he asked.

François and Angelique, waiting in a secluded alcove, waved us closer. I let go of Tudor's hand and went to them. I gave Angelique a big hug, feeling so relieved to see her healthy again. I could feel her love and concern as she hugged me back. I embraced François, my vampire ex-beau and former lover, and placed a soft kiss on his lips. I felt his strong arms and felt instantly safe and secure.

"Hello, *chérie*. I've missed you," he whispered in my ear.

I'd missed him, too, and I was glad to see him, except that I was self-conscious at that moment in Tudor's presence. François was a gorgeous French vampire, and he was my friend, and in the past I had made love to him willingly. Behind me stood Tudor, my new lover, who was waiting with trepidation to find out who the gorgeous man I had just kissed and embraced was. A rival? I was caught between two lovers who didn't know each other, one a vampire and the other a human, both of them doctors.

"And you must be the Dr. Tudor I have heard so much about," said Angelique suavely, approaching Tudor and easing the awkwardness.

There was no need to delay the introductions. Hopefully, there weren't going to be any unanswerable questions coming from Tudor.

I inhaled to muster my courage and said, "Yes, Angelique and François, this is Dr. Tudor Lupu, a new friend I've made here in Romania. Tudor, this is Angelique Brazeau and this is Dr. François Le Beau, my best friends."

Angelique did not hesitate to give Tudor a tender hug. "Tudor—may I call you Tudor? Of course I can. Any of Cat's friends is my friend as well. Oh my, you look adorable." She stood back to admire a completely embarrassed and red-faced Tudor.

"Nice to meet you, Angelique," he said, looking intently at her. She would be the first woman vampire he ever met.

François and Tudor shook hands. Suspecting a possible adversary, Tudor locked steely eyes on him, while François seemed relaxed and half-amused for reasons of his own.

"Doctor," said François.

"Doctor," replied Tudor, wincing at the cold, hard hand he was shaking. He then turned to me and asked, "How good of a friend is Dr. François to you, Cat?"

I understood the intonation in his question, and I tried to formulate a satisfactory answer, but François came to my rescue.

"We are just good friends, Dr. Lupu. You don't have to worry about us or me." François smiled sincerely at him.

"Call me Tudor." I could hear the relief in Tudor's voice.

"Call me François."

"So both of you are vampires as well?" Tudor asked to be sure, because both Angelique and François, at a closer inspection in the daylight coming through the nearby windows, looked human, though pale.

"Yes, we are." François' smile disappeared, but he kept a pleasant disposition. "Mundibuto, who I believe you've met, told me what happened recently in Sighisoara."

"That's why you're here?" I interjected.

"Yes."

"Where is Mundibuto?" I looked around, expecting to see him.

"Presently, Mundibuto is on a discovery mission," answered Angelique. "However, we're not in the right place to discuss this subject. There are two agents who are following you. I think you know them—Dorin and Stanca Ionescu." She looked from me to Tudor.

"That was to be expected. They are from the Romanian Secret Service, and they'd been with us in Sighisoara. But if they're following us, I didn't spot them."

"They have electronic surveillance on your car, and they are keeping at a safe distance," said François.

"Take this, hon, and we can talk while separated from each other." Angelique handed me a Bluetooth earpiece with a microphone and a communicator device, similar to what we had used in New York when we were trying to avoid the NSA.

I placed the Bluetooth device on my ear, covered it with my blonde locks, and turned the communicator on. "Where shall we go?"

I heard in my ear, "Continue your tour. We'll be nearby."

"Where are they?" Tudor wondered, turning around and looking for them. In the moment it took for Tudor to glance at me as I was mounting my earpiece, the vampires had vanished. "One minute they're here, the next they're gone as if they've disappeared into thin air."

"Don't worry. They're around." I pointed to my ear. "I'll need to talk to them.

"OK, François and Angelique, what's going on?"

"Cat, we arrived from New York yesterday." I heard François's voice. "Mundibuto told us about the army of proto-vampires and zombies that Eleonore had amassed and that you destroyed. And you got rid of three bad vampires. You've done well, *chérie*."

"Thanks. I had lots of help, you know. But tell me, why are you and Angelique here?"

"Mundibuto has snooped around and thinks the queen is up to major merde. She has many more vampires serving her, and we need to join forces and find out what she's plotting."

"Is it that serious?"

"Yes. What are your plans after today, hon?" asked Angelique this time.

"Tudor and I?"

"Yes."

"After today, we were going to drive back to Timisoara and see other historic sites on the way, including the Corvin Castle."

"Get away from this area, hon. And try to avoid that castle."

I frowned. Something serious was going down, and they wanted us away from the heart of Transylvania. "Where do you expect to find the queen?"

"Probably in some cave in the Carpathian Mountains," replied François.

"That won't be difficult, will it?"

"There are only several hundred caves, at least those the geologists know about."

"What makes you think she's in a cave? You, Angelique, and Mundibuto are not hiding in caves."

"True. If she were by herself, we would find her in a castle or a mountain retreat, but based on what you saw under the cemetery in Sighisoara, we think she has another similar base camp, only bigger."

I motioned with my head to Tudor that we needed to leave. He was curious about what I was talking to François about, but he didn't ask any questions.

As we walked to the exit, I continued my conversation with François. "What do you want me to do?"

"Go back to New York, *chérie*. You'll be safer there."

"And leave you three here alone?"

"I know that you have your Strigoi, and they can protect you, but you cannot fight vampires, and we expect many of them."

This sounded to me like big trouble, but there wasn't much I could do. Queen Eleonore von Schwarzenberg, a vampire and the self-appointed queen of vampires, was not going to throw her hands up and surrender because three vampires, friends of my late great-great-grandfather Vlad V, were going to demand she comply with the unwritten rule prohibiting vampire intervention in human affairs. She had violated that law by converting many humans into proto-vampires—beasts that were neither human nor vampire but bloodthirsty cannibals. She also had created zombies from dead people. All in all, she had sinister plans, and she had her own vampires to protect her.

If she didn't agree to Mundibuto, Angelique, and François's demands, there was going to be a war, and I was not sure if my friends would win or if I'd ever see them alive again. Worry clouded my eyes, and Tudor put his arms around me, visibly concerned. This was not an issue he needed to know about, nor was it an issue that would affect him. But in my case, although I was not a vampire, this conflict in the vampire world was my concern. What could I do about it?

"François, I cannot turn tail and run—"

"You must, *chérie*. This confrontation might get deadly."

"I am the great-great-granddaughter of Vlad V Draculesti. I'll think of something." I ended the communication.

Chapter 3. Cat

Tudor had his arm around my shoulder. I circled my arm around his waist and leaned my head on his chest. "We need to get back to Timisoara."

"Sure. What's the matter? Problems with that queen?"

I nodded, deep in thought.

"Let's go then."

Holding each other close, we exited Bran Castle, descended to the bottom of the hill, and returned to our rented car.

When we were inside the car, Tudor asked me, "Are you in danger?"

"I don't think so, but it's better to get out of here before there's trouble."

"I gather you want to go straight back and you don't want to see any other historical sights or the Corvin Castle?"

"Right. Let's go back to Timisoara," I said darkly.

Tudor drove away, but he kept looking in the rearview mirror, checking for possible pursuers.

"Don't worry, they're following us from a distance," I told him. "This car has a radio tracker attached to it somewhere."

"Yes, you're right. Not to mention being tracked by our mobile phones." He gave me his phone and I removed the battery, and then I did the same on mine.

"Are Dorin and Stanca following us?" Tudor asked.

"Probably, but that is the least of our problems. I'm worried about Queen Eleonore and her vampires."

"Is that what your friend François told you?"

"Yes, but most likely she's not after us. Yet. My friends are searching for her to find out why she built that army. And there will be trouble—big, big trouble—when they encounter her."

"Can you tell me what's going on?"

"Yes, but you must not divulge what I tell you." I looked pleadingly at him.

"On my honor."

"There is an unwritten law among the vampires that they will not infect humans and make them vampires unless absolutely necessary."

"Really? Why?"

"If vampirism spreads in the world, it will mean the end of humanity and, eventually, of the vampires as well."

"Fascinating. And it makes sense."

"Most vampires understand that they are human mutants. Not one of them was born a vampire, and they don't want to spread their curse. They want to live quiet lives and remain undiscovered. Occasionally, someone like Eleonore has illusions of grandeur and wants to become the ruler of the world. And that would be the end of all of us."

"Yes, I can see how being a vampire and living forever would be very attractive to most people," said Tudor. "It could become an irreversible pandemic, and once all humans became vampires, they in turn would die without human blood. I'm glad that there are some vampires who are thinking the right way."

"Now you see the predicament we're in. The knowledge that vampires exist and who they are cannot be divulged to humanity."

"Except that you and I are humans, and we know about them," said Tudor. "What's in store for us?"

"Nothing, as long as we keep our mouths shut."

"For some reason, I don't fear your friends, Cat. I'm afraid of the queen."

"So am I. That's why we're leaving."

"Let me understand this: The queen must have subjects, other vampires, right?"

"Yes."

"How many vampires, besides your friends Mundibuto, Angelique, and François, are out there?"

"From what I've read in my great-great-grandfather's records, there should be a few dozen or so, but I don't know exactly how many they are. That's why I'm afraid for my friends, although they are strong, smart, and quick. But they are only three against God knows how many of Eleonore's vampires."

Tudor gave a long, apprehensive whistle. "Is there anything we can do?"

I shook my head and sighed.

"How do you feel about all this?"

"Tormented about running away and leaving them on their own."

"We could ask for help from the Romanian authorities—" He saw my worried face and added, "Not a good idea."

After a long, silent drive, Tudor said, "May I ask you about François?"

"Sure. What do you want to know?"

"Were you intimate with him?"

I looked at him and he looked back at me. I wasn't going to lie. "Yes."

"Do you have feelings for him?"

"Yes, I love him, but—"

"But?"

"I also love you, Tudor."

He almost lost control of the car. After he regained his composure, he pulled onto a dirt side road. "Explain, please. Because I have strong feelings for you, and I'm kind of scared that I'll lose you to him."

How could I explain that I loved two men at the same time in a way that wouldn't make Tudor walk away? Tudor was a great man, and I'd had fallen in love with him in the short time we'd been together.

"First, François is a vampire. He has been that way for about 100 years. He saved my life, and he's my hero," I said.

Tudor looked puzzled.

"He saved my life," I repeated, and touched my cross pendant on my neck. "I was about to be brutally raped and murdered when he came to my rescue. But that's not the reason I love him. I feel that he cares for me."

"Does he love you?"

"I think so. As much as a vampire can love, I suppose."

"Vampires are not capable of love?" Tudor asked, with hope in his voice.

"Yes, they are, but they must meet the right woman or man. They know that they will live for a long time, and the ones they love will age and die one day. They are reluctant to attach themselves to mortals." I sighed.

"And I have my own pragmatic view of such a relationship," I continued. "He is a vampire and I am a human. Other than a carnal attraction between us, there couldn't be any future for us. I cannot have children with him, and I will age and eventually die, while he will continue to live on and stay young and gorgeous. I had a fling with him and I love him, but..."

Tudor picked up my thought. "As a human, you cannot see a future with him."

I shook my head, and tears streaked down my cheeks. I leaned over and Tudor took me into his arms. I felt his sincere love and caring for me.

"I love you, Cat. And I'd like to be with you for a long time." He rubbed my tears away with his thumbs.

I lifted my head to him and we kissed tenderly. I was lucky—or cursed—to love and be loved by two gorgeous men, one human and the other a vampire. "I'm sorry if I've disappointed you."

"I'm glad you came into my life, Cat." He held my chin up and looked into my eyes. His emerald-green eyes were so comforting, I couldn't resist— I lowered the seat back and pulled him on top of me.

He reached down, lifted my skirt, and pulled my panties off. I unbuckled his belt and lowered his pants and shorts, as we kissed breathlessly. He thrust himself inside me, and I was in heaven.

We climaxed at the same time. We were breathing heavily from our short but intense sexual encounter when we heard a police siren that gave us a quick wake-up call.

Chapter 4. Cat

Tudor raised his head and said, "Oh, crap. The cops." He returned quickly to the driver's seat and managed to pull his pants up and buckle his belt. I raised the back of my seat, lowered my skirt, and hastily put my sunglasses on.

The policeman sauntered toward our rental car.

Tudor lowered his window. "Good day, Officer," he said cheerily in English.

I looked ahead, pretending not to notice the cop.

"Good day, sir. May I see your driver's license, insurance card, and registration, please?"

"Sure, but what seems to be the trouble?" Tudor said innocently, while reaching for his wallet. He pulled out several cards, including one with a red cross, showing he was a doctor. "By the way, I'm Dr. Lupu."

The cop inspected the documents and took a long look at him, realizing that he was a Romanian. He waved the card with the Red Cross on it and continued in English, "Well, Doctor, you should be aware that performing lascivious acts on the side of the highway is a misdemeanor, subject to fines and/or imprisonment."

Tudor rubbed the bridge of his nose. "Lascivious acts? That sounds serious. Officer, we were just resting for a few minutes here on this dirt road, away from the main highway."

"Resting, eh?" He looked around. "I suppose you're far enough away from the highway. And since I didn't catch you in the act, I'll let you go with a warning." He handed the documents back to Tudor.

"Thank you, Officer." Tudor returned the cards to his wallet.

"Which way were you going?"

"West," said Tudor.

"You may want to go through Hunedoara and take E79. The highway E673 to Timisoara is blocked at Deva due to some emergency repairs, and it is very slow."

"Thank you, Officer, I'll follow your advice."

The cop bent down to take a good look at me. He said, "Have a nice day, and do try to give a good example to our young citizens." He saluted and returned to his car.

Tudor did not linger and drove away. As soon as we were back on the highway, both of us exploded in laughter. It felt good to do naughty things and to get away with them without being caught *in flagrante delicto*.

"Dr. Lupu—shame, shame, shame on you for taking advantage of a young lady on the side of the road with a total disregard for the young citizens," I teased him.

"I take full responsibility, young lady," he said, feigning humility.

"So you tried to impress on the cop that you are a doctor."

"It worked, didn't it?"

"Or maybe he didn't see anything suspicious," I said, hoping that he didn't see us making passionate love in the car in broad daylight.

"Oh, I think he saw what he needed to see. He encounters these 'lascivious acts' every day."

"Including by doctors?"

He turned red. "I'm sorry, I couldn't help it."

I stroked the back of his neck. "I'm not. I liked it."

"Me, too." He beamed as if he were a kid who'd eaten a chocolate cookie and gotten away with it.

"I need to stop at a restroom," I said.

He nodded. "It seems that we may see the Corvin Castle after all."

"Hmm?" I remembered Angelique saying we should avoid the Corvin Castle.

"The detour will put us within sight of the castle. It will not be much of a delay, and it is a beautiful castle."

I thought about it. It would still be full daylight when we arrived there. "Let's make that decision when we get there."

Chapter 5. The Vampires

After meeting Cat in the Bran Castle, François and Angelique returned to Rasnov to meet their friend Mundibuto, the black vampire. They pulled their car up alongside Mundibuto's in a parking lot below Rasnov's famous fortress on the hill. Mundibuto, sporting an African skullcap over his shaved head, was leaning against his car, waiting for them. They joined him, quickly eyeing their surroundings.

"How is she?" Mundibuto asked.

"Surprisingly well, after what she's been through," Angelique replied.

"My potion is still working," said Mundibuto, referring to the voodoo tonic he'd given Cat a few months earlier. The potion was to protect her from an emotional breakdown following her being kidnapped, almost raped and killed, and then witnessing François rip the assailants' throats with his fangs. "And if it weren't for her in the crypt, I might not be here today. She is a Draculesti to the core, and she's not even a vampire. Yet."

Angelique and François looked at him with mixed emotions. Cat was the only non-vampire who knew so much about vampires. Her vampire friends trusted her, although she had killed two vampires, Fakeula and Nicolae, a feat not many mortals could claim. And those two vampires—along with Ilie, who was killed by Mundibuto— deserved death. Nicolae and Ilie were two of the traitors who had helped the Turkish assassins behead Vlad the Impaler, Vlad V's uncle. Cat had nicknamed the vampire Fakeula because he resembled a young Vlad V, a fake-

Dracula. He, along with Nicolae and Ilie, were the custodians of an army of proto-vampires and zombies kept in hibernation in a catacomb under the hill cemetery in Sighisoara. Cat, Mundibuto, and Tudor had managed to destroy them. And consequently, Cat and Tudor, two mortals, were deeply involved in a new vampire war that was about to erupt.

Fakeula, Nicolae, and Ilie were Queen Eleonore's subjects, and she would not be happy about the demise of her subjects and her army. In fact, she would be murderously pissed. It was very important for François, Mundibuto, and Angelique to end her aspirations, perhaps even kill her quickly and prevent more humans from getting involved and potentially exposing the vampire society to the world. Sending Cat and Tudor out of the area near Sighisoara, where the queen was believed to live, was the prudent thing to do.

"How do you feel about Cat and Tudor?" Angelique asked François.

"What?" He was surprised by the question.

"You know..." Angelique could not say the rest. Mundibuto looked away.

"That Cat and Tudor are romantically involved?" François raised an eyebrow. "Yes, I knew at first glance when I saw them in Bran Castle." François shrugged. "What do you expect? Tudor is a handsome, warm-blooded man, and if it brings happiness to Cat, I'm OK with it."

"You'll not kill Tudor, will you?" Angelique asked sharply. Mundibuto stared at François now.

"No," François said. "Not unless he divulges our secret."

Angelique narrowed her eyes at François suspiciously.

"Yes, I love Cat, as I haven't loved a mortal woman since I was a mortal myself," said François. "But I don't kill my rivals over any woman. And in this case I have to face reality. Cat is a mortal and I am a vampire. She will age and die. I will continue to be young for a long time. Not to mention that we won't be able to have children, and most women want children. Isn't that right, Angelique?"

She nodded, thinking of her past as a mortal woman. "Although I had forgone children to be Maurice's mistress, I had hopes that one day I could have children with him." Angelique remembered her lover from 200 years ago in France and later in Egypt.

"Then you see that I haven't any right to interfere in Cat's life. We couldn't have a future, and I wish her well. I'll always be her friend." François turned his head away and ran his fingers through his silver-blond hair.

Angelique came to him and circled her arms around him, leaning her head on his chest. "You're a good vampire, François."

Mundibuto smirked. "Enough with this mushy stuff. We've got work to do."

"You're right, Mundibuto. What did you discover while we were talking to Cat?" François asked.

"The good news is that I found two strong leads to the queen's den, but—"

"But?" wondered François.

"She may have dozens of vampires with her. We're outnumbered."

"First, let's find her whereabouts. We're not going to drop into her court without a plan or an offer that she refuses at her own peril," François said.

Angelique and Mundibuto agreed.

"In the meanwhile, I have a shipment of heavy-caliber weapons and grenade-launchers coming from Ukraine."

"Couldn't you get weapons locally, here in Romania?" Angelique asked.

François shook his head. "Ukraine is in chaos. They'll sell you anything you want there. Delivery is expected in two days."

"So," said Mundibuto. "Back to the leads I found. One is inside the Rasnov Fortress." He pointed to the high walls of the fortress above them. "The other is south, in the mountains above Bran Castle."

"We just came from there," Angelique said.

Mundibuto shook his head. "Not at Bran Castle, but up in the rocky peaks above Bran. There is a cave there, not well-known and not easily accessible."

"How did you find these leads?" François asked.

Mundibuto opened a small stainless steel container and handed it to François. "In there are the ashes of the zombies and the proto-vampires we destroyed in the catacombs under Sighisoara cemetery."

François smelled the contents and turned away quickly. He gave the container to Angelique, who, after having a sniff, closed the container with a disgusted look.

"Did it smell that way in there, in the catacombs?" Angelique asked.

"No, not at first," said Mundibuto. "It seems that a substance that may have been in the bodies of the zombies and proto-vampires became unstable by the next day, when I went back for some more cleanup. Even a vampire couldn't stand the stench, and I had to return with a gas mask. After I turned on a yellow spectrum light to help me spot any traces of the blue blood left by the decapitated vampires, I saw the ashes irradiating in the ultraviolet spectrum."

"You followed the trails?" François asked.

Mundibuto nodded. "While waiting for you to arrive, I followed both of them. One leads to the Rasnov Fortress and the other to the cave up there." He gestured toward the rocky peaks of the Carpathian Mountains in the distance. "I didn't go inside either one of them."

"Where did the trail originate?" François asked, furrowing his eyebrows.

"The trails seemed to be linked, although one disappears over the highway connection bctwccn Bran and Rasnov."

"It would appear that she uses vehicles to transport them," said Angelique. "She could come from anywhere in Transylvania to visit these two sites."

"Yeah, that's what I figured," said Mundibuto. "But it won't be long before she discovers the annihilation we caused in Sighisoara. If we find similar sites here under

Rasnov and in the cave up there, and if she doesn't currently occupy any of them, she will come visiting soon." Mundibuto crossed his massive arms and smiled evilly.

"In that case, we will do reconnaissance first," said François. "We'll need the weapons when the time comes to negotiate with her."

"So, until the weapons arrive, we have two days to learn what we can before facing her majesty," said Angelique with a snarl. "By the way, isn't there a cave nearby here, too?"

"Yes, there is a cave in that direction." Mundibuto pointed to a spot along the highway. "It is clean. No traces there." He pointed to three large bags in the back of his car. "I've brought all the equipment we need for exploration."

"OK, there are three of us and two points of interest." François looked from the fortress to the peaks in the distance.

"And two days to find out what's going on before the shooting starts," said Angelique. "I'll go with François to the cave in the Carpathian Mountains. Rasnov is yours, Mundibuto."

Without another word, Angelique and François removed two bags from Mundibuto's car and placed them in their car. After they obtained the GPS coordinates from Mundibuto, they parted company.

Chapter 6. Mundibuto

Mundibuto returned to the town of Rasnov to wait for the sunset. He took the time to refuel his body with *palinča*, the Transylvanian plum brandy that can burn a mortal's guts, at an outdoor café overlooking the fortress on the hill. Entering the fortress after dark would be easier and would raise less suspicion from the locals.

The sun had already set when Mundibuto hiked the hill to the fortress. He jumped over the high walls in one leap and ended up near the small village enclosed within the fortress's walls. Some people were still in the souvenir stores housed inside the medieval stone houses, so he moved stealthily to the well of the fortress. The well was 450 feet deep; legend had it that, centuries ago, Turkish prisoners taken captive after an assault on the fortress dug the well out of solid rock. They died digging the well, and water was found in an underground river. Where there is underground flowing water, there are caves, and that's what Mundibuto was interested in exploring.

The well was no longer in use. Mundibuto pulled out two of the several planks that covered the well and squeezed himself and his bag through the gap. After pulling the planks back over the top of the well, he assessed the deep round shaft he was in. At the top, the well's walls were covered by green moss. Moving like a spider down the walls, he descended to the dank, dark bottom. Although it was pitch black, which was not a disadvantage for a vampire, he turned on his small headlamp that emitted the yellow spectrum to detect any ultraviolet traces left by zombies or proto-vampires. The walls of the well were immediately illuminated in an indigo hue visible only to a vampire.

Mundibuto crawled inside the narrow tunnel and assessed the exploration possibilities. The indigo hue was nowhere to be seen. The tunnel must have been flooded during the spring runoffs and washed clean of any traces of the substance he was looking for. The tunnel was just large enough for him to crawl through on all fours. He decided to explore the downstream route and soon came to a mass of stones and gravel that closed off the tunnel. Over millennia, the runoffs had carried debris that blocked the tunnel, allowing only water to pass through, which eventually surfaced above the ground into the nearby valley.

Straddling the small stream, he reversed direction and began exploring upstream. After several hundred feet of dark, tight passages, he found a vertical crack in the stone that opened up into a larger opening. The water must have carved the underground crevice in the bedrock. Now Mundibuto could walk upright most of the time. The narrow, slightly sloping cave continued meandering inside the mountain, ascending toward the Carpathians. Mundibuto sniffed the air carefully as he progressed deeper, smelling for either carbon dioxide or methane gas. Over a period of time, a lack of oxygen would be deadly, even for a vampire. The air was humid but OK to breathe. To his satisfaction, the indigo hue appeared at times on the walls of this underground river cave. He was on the right track.

In a larger chamber, adorned with several stalactites and stalagmites, the underground river bifurcated. A smaller stream came from his right, through what seemed to be a cave-in of rocks from long ago. Mundibuto speculated that it could have been a branch connecting to the Rasnov Valley Cave, a few kilometers from the fort. It was a dead end, but he heard faint music coming from the cracks in the blockage. He perked up his ears, puzzled at what he was hearing. It was classical music. Curious, he began dislodging a few rocks to get closer to the source of the music. He found a crevice at the top of the rubble large enough to squeeze through without his backpack, and he crawled along the fissure, which cut through the solid rock. As he crept along, advancing on his belly, the music got louder. Then suddenly, to his surprise, the music stopped and applause followed.

Classical music and applause was coming from somewhere above him. The faint smell of candle wax infused the air. He pushed his way farther and after several minutes, he reached the end of the crevice. There, a narrow vertical crack was lit by soft light. He pushed to get as close as he could to spy through the crack. The music started anew as he stretched his neck and looked through the narrow opening with only one eye. He saw a large cave. Down on the stone floor, among the stalagmites, a conductor was leading an orchestra in a Haydn concerto. There was no electric lighting, just dozen of candles illuminating the cave. The audience sat in a semicircle, listening and sipping champagne. Mundibuto licked his lips and blinked dumbly. This was unusual—a concert being performed in the cave.

The crack in the crevice was not large enough for him to see much of the strange concert. Luckily, he had his phone with him, and after some contortions, he pulled it out of his pocket, extended his hand, and snapped several pictures through the narrow opening. He viewed the photos and shook his head, annoyed that he had crawled all the way here to see spectators dressed in 18th-century attire and white powdered wigs, listening to Haydn. It must have been just a costume show for the amusement of classical music aficionados. Not wanting to waste any more time, he slowly pushed himself back through the crack he had come through.

Something nagged at him, though. Why the 18th century? What had happened in the 18th century?

Chapter 7. Mundibuto

The trail continued along the left fork of the underground creek up to a point where the water gushed through small cracks that were impassable. But it was not a dead end. Just to the right, a narrow corridor cut into the stone and continued going up. The indigo traces were clear indications of a trail to a camp possibly occupied by more zombies and proto-vampires. The narrow passage angled to the left and dropped down several feet after which, just as abruptly, it regained its previous level, continuing into an upside down V-shaped passage. He hopped over this unexpected trench and continued walking on a bed of gravel formed by an ancient underground river. A human skeleton, hung from the narrow ceiling by a thick rope blocked the passage a few yards into the tunnel.

Mundibuto smirked. Living in Africa for the past century had prepared him to recognize methods of terrifying trespassers or setting deadly traps for the wanted or unwanted, man or beast. The skeleton was a warning to go no farther, except that a gold chain dangled around the skeleton's neck, tempting the greedy to pull it off. He knew better and looked carefully at the back of the necklace. It was attached to a small chain that paralleled the thick rope supporting the skeleton from the narrow ceiling. A large stalactite hung menacingly at the top. Pull the gold necklace and the stalactite would come down, crushing an intruder's head.

Going around it was not possible. The skeleton and the rope blocked the passage. Passing underneath was not possible, either, as two smaller chains attached to the ankles held the skeleton in place like a macabre gate. It was well rigged, as all the bones were wired to each other to act as a deadly barrier. Move the skeleton or pull the gold necklace off, and the stalactite would come down like a guillotine. Mundibuto stepped back, picked up a rock, and threw it at the skeleton's chest. With a loud screech, the stalactite plummeted, crushing the skeleton and any potential trespasser as well.

And that was that, thought Mundibuto—but it wasn't. The stalactite or something else triggered another trap, and this one was far deadlier. Two slabs of rock, one ahead of him and the other behind, slammed down, entrapping Mundibuto in a stone cell. Mundibuto cursed in as many African languages as he knew, but that did not help him. There was no way out.

The trap was a sophisticated, man-made—or vampire-made—mechanism intended to kill or take captive any intruders. His only hope now was that someone, perhaps the master of this stone trap, would be alerted and come to check on him. He didn't have to wait long. Above him, a stone hatch was pulled back, and soft light poured through the square opening. The curly, beehived, white-wigged head of a woman peered down through the stone window. She focused on him down below and smirked.

"Hello!" Mundibuto waved at her. "Can you help me get out of this predicament?"

"Ahh, we've caught a black rat," said the pompously coiffured woman in German-accented English. "And in one piece, nonetheless." She giggled gaily.

"Who the hell are you?"

"For your information, commoner, I am Queen Eleonore von Schwarzenberg."

His eyes opened wide in surprise. "You're the queen?" She was a mortal back in the 18th century, but now she was a vampire. He hadn't known what Queen Eleonore von Schwarzenberg looked like, and if this really were her, she had trapped him instead of him trapping her.

"That's right." She nodded slowly, and her wig followed the motion. "You may address me as 'your majesty'."

"Careful with that beehive wig of yours. Don't drop it." That was the best Mundibuto could say, as his mind clouded over with fury and anger.

"You are just an African savage, but you'll change your tune soon."

Mundibuto looked at his stone cell. He was her prisoner. "OK, lady. What's the meaning of this? Why am I trapped in here? A man can't even explore a cave nowadays?"

"I ask the questions. Why are you, a black man, exploring an unknown cave in the Carpathians?"

"You know, I'm going to sue you for endangering my life. You're going to hear from my lawyer." He shook an indignant finger at her, and since she didn't know who he was, he acted as if he were just another blundering tourist with civil rights.

"Who are you? What's your name?" she asked.

"George Washington, the famous cave explorer."

"Please. Do you think I was born yesterday?"

True, thought Mundibuto; she had to have been born before George Washington.

"How did you get in here?" she asked.

"Through the underground river, near Rasnov."

"That passage was blocked a century ago. The only access is either through the well in the Rasnov Fortress or through the western access. Considering the location of your bag, you came through the well. How did you know about that entrance?"

"I told you, I came through an underground river," said Mundibuto.

The queen scrutinized him. "You're big, and you are not a cave explorer. What's in your bag?"

"Open this trap and I'll show you." Mundibuto unzipped the bag, reaching for his gun. But then he reconsidered. Even if he shot her, she wouldn't die. He pulled out instead a green, Nigerian passport.

"Easy there," said the queen, furrowing her brow.

"Just my proof of identity." He waved it in the air.

"George Washington with a Nigerian passport," she said suspiciously. Her vampire vision had no problem spotting the passport issuer even in the dim light cast from behind her. "Tell me your true identity and your business here before I flood the rat hole you're in."

"Listen, your majesty—"

"You're a vampire," Eleonore cut him off, as she finally realized whom she had in her possession. "A black vampire. You are Mundibuto, aren't you?"

He hadn't wanted to divulge his identity so soon. Now that Eleonore knew who he was, the game had changed.

"Vlady told me that Nicolae and Ilie threw you into a deep hole. How did you get out?" She began screaming, "Where are Vlady, Nicolae, and Ilie? What did you do to them?"

He realized that she didn't know yet what had happened to her vampire subjects and the army under the cemetery in Sighisoara. That gave him some time before she unleashed her wrath on him once she found out that her army had been pulverized.

"So you know who I am." He pulled his phone from his pocket and checked the pictures he had taken in the concert cave. There she was, Eleonore in her baby-blue silk evening gown and two-foot-tall hairdo, sitting prim and proper, enjoying the Haydn concerto in a cave. He wished he had known what she looked like before he took the picture. He would have been more cautious or, better yet, he would have stopped the search, gotten out, and captured her. "What do you want?"

"What did you do with Vlady, Nicolae, and Ilie?" Her voice was sharper than a knife.

He figured that Vlady must have been Fakeula, whom Cat had nicknamed.

"Your subjects, your majesty, are in a safe place." He decided to lie. "If you want them, let me go."

"I hope for your sake they are alive and well," she said coldly. "However, in the meantime, I have to attend to apprehending your two friends."

"Who?" he asked unsure of whom of his two friends she was talking about.

"Catherina Sanders, the great-great-granddaughter of Vlad V, and her friend—what's his name—yes, Dr. Tudor Lupu."

"The hell you will!" Mundibuto leaped up to grab Eleonore by the neck, but she, too, was a vampire. She quickly pulled her head back in, but not before losing her wig to Mundibuto's fingers. He discarded the wig and reached up through the opening, holding on its ledge, looking at her with murderous eyes.

She stood back from his reach. Without her towering wig, Eleonore looked less than regal, and her expression was toxic. "Let's get something clear, you big black brute. You are my prisoner." She continued in a cheerier voice, "Let me put it this way. I have good news and better news. The good news is that I'll come back to interrogate you thoroughly and find out what the hell happened in Sighisoara. The better news is that I may not be tempted to make you my subject but to let you die in there like a rat. Bye-bye." She waved at him and the stone hatch slammed shut, pushing his fingers from the sill.

He dropped down to the gravel floor but jumped up again, propping himself against the narrowly spaced walls, and he began pounding on the stone hatch. The granite hatch did not budge.

Down at the bottom, he paced back and forth like a caged tiger. He was beyond furious that he had failed, that he had been caught, that he had underestimated this queen bitch. And he couldn't do a thing about it but wait for her to return.

Chapter 8. François and Angelique

François and Angelique drove as far as they could off the main highway onto a dirt road leading up into the mountains. The road ended in a primitive campsite, which was deserted. They left the car at the camp and, following the GPS coordinates, they hiked higher up through the pinewoods along a canyon. They followed an old established path that seemed to lead toward the cave. François had consulted a map earlier to identify the cave they were seeking, but the cave was not registered as a major cave, so it must have been more like a grotto. That, however, did not discourage them, as they occasionally spotted faint traces of indigo hue along the trail. Just below where the forest line ended, they came upon the cave, which was just a grotto, as the map had suggested. From all indications, campers would spend nights here and possibly, in the winter, animals might call the place home.

"There's nothing here," said Angelique, inspecting the grotto.

François turned on his yellow-light lamp, and inescapable traces of indigo hue covered the left side of the wall. The traces ended abruptly near the ceiling of the grotto.

"That's where the entrance is," he said, smiling. "It is perfectly camouflaged near the ceiling. No wonder people couldn't find it."

"Or maybe the bat dung discouraged anyone from looking further." Just as Angelique said that, a stream of bats flew out from the unseen opening and into the dusky

sky. She covered her head with her hands to prevent them from getting tangled up in her hair.

François sat against the wall on the opposite side, away from the main path of the flying creatures, and said, "We'll have to wait until the cave is empty of bats."

Two hours later, most of the bats were out hunting for insects. A few stragglers came out now and then, but it was safe to explore the interior.

"What do you think?" Angelique asked, standing up, dusting her pants.

"It will take a precise jump," said François, looking up. "It's about twenty feet up, with only a three-to four-foot hidden opening, just below the ceiling."

François hoisted the pack off his back and, in one leap, reached the opening above. With one hand, he grasped a hidden edge while he propped the other on the ceiling to keep from bumping his head on it.

He climbed in quickly and a minute later, his head appeared above the threshold of the entrance. "This is the real thing, Angelique. Toss me the bags and then jump up. Oh, and be careful. It is pretty slick and smelly up here."

"Just what a lady needs, to crawl in bat shit." After tossing the bags to François, she leaped, locked hands with François, and with one swift movement, he pulled her in. "Crap. You were not kidding. I hope there's some water inside the cave." Angelique walked on her tiptoes, too disgusted to touch anything, and she followed François, who was carrying the bags.

Although at first the entrance corridor was relatively small, it soon opened into a large chamber, which may have been formed from a shift in the mountain's rock plates. François and Angelique turned their yellow lights on, and the indigo hue continued on the path down inside the mountain. The ceiling of the chamber held a few more squeaking bats too lazy to have flown out for dinner.

"I'm glad we're getting away from this place." Repulsed, Angelique followed François down the path.

There were many side chambers and fissures leading in all directions from the path they walked on, which was well demarcated by the indigo hue left behind by the zombies. But the dry cave they explored soon came to an abrupt end.

"Here is the first trap," said François, pointing to a vertical shaft dropping into oblivion. "The access is above and behind. Almost impossible to detect." He shone his light above, where violet-hued traces showed the true path.

He jumped, reached up, and pulled himself inside another cavity, after which he popped his head out and said, "Throw me the bags."

Angelique complied and then she, too, followed the same routine to reach the upper but well-hidden crevice, which sloped upward but quickly descended again, opening into a wet cave ornamented with the typical stalactites and stalagmites. The yellow lights from their lamps cast long and narrow shadows on the walls as they continued descending. Eventually, they encountered a small stream of water, and they both washed the smeared dung from their shoes and hands.

"I don't understand—why come all the way here, into the middle of a mountain?" Angelique wondered while shaking her hands dry.

"You mean, why this deep inside the mountain?"

"Exactly. You can hide anywhere above ground. Eleonore had already found a good place to hide her army in Sighisoara, under the cemetery. Why come here?"

"That's what we'll find out," said François.

"Have you ever met Eleonore?"

"A couple of times, early in the 20th century," he said. "She's an aristocrat from a noble family, but she's not exactly endearing. I never thought she would be capable of what Mundibuto told us."

"I wonder if Vlad knew about this," she said.

"His ashes and the Strigoi destroyed her army. He had to have had at least a suspicion." François referred to the ghostly entities that Cat had inherited from Vlad V to protect her.

"I've seen what the Strigoi can do. Cat unleashed them at the Silver Coffin Nightclub in New York, but considering that they are useless against vampires, it makes me wonder about Vlad's frame of mind. He sent Cat to a certain death in Transylvania."

"And yet, Cat destroyed the queen's army and killed two full-fledged vampires."

"That's true." Angelique thought for a moment. "Do you think Vlad wanted Cat to become a vampire?"

François looked at Angelique for a long time and then said, "He gave her that option, and if she wishes, she could become one of us. It is in her power to do so."

"How? Do you mean to say that Vlad asked you to turn her into a vampire, if needed?"

François scratched his head, a habit left from his human days. "Well, I might as well tell you this in case Cat becomes incapacitated and her life—"

"What?" Angelique was fearful of what she might hear.

"Vlad gave Cat an ampule of his blue blood."

"Huh?"

"Yes, and I inserted the ampule behind her right ear. At any time she chooses, she can open the ampule and she will become a vampire. But again—only if she so wishes."

"Wow! That's...that's unexpected," said Angelique, recovering from her shock. "And Vlad gave her that choice?"

François nodded.

"Mundibuto and I became vampires because we were infected by the Egyptian vampire strain," she said, almost to herself. "But you, François, thanks to Dr. Hellinherr Sr., became a proto-vampire, and Vlad had no choice but to transform you into a vampire. I don't know of anyone he willingly changed into a vampire. Except now for Cat, by giving her that option."

"That's not exactly true." François saw the bafflement on Angelique's face. "Vlad transformed Eleonore into a vampire."

"Say what? Why?"

"It's kind of a long story, but he owed his life to her."

Angelique looked even more puzzled.

"And Eleonore was dying of cancer."

"So?" Angelique's eyebrows wrinkled.

"It might have been an amorous fling, too."

"Men. Even vampire men are the same." She shook her head, half-amused, half-disappointed. "Then why did he give Cat the choice to become a vampire?"

"Vlad expected troubled times ahead of us, and he wanted Cat to be protected if needed."

"Like what we will find in here." Angelique pointed down the path leading deeper into the mountain.

"Yep. And maybe more," acknowledged François. "Let's see what we find at the end of this hell hole." His foot fell through the seemingly solid rock, sinking down to his knee. He felt a metallic click under his foot and raised his hand to stop Angelique from coming to his aid.

"Angelique, I think I just stepped on a landmine or some kind of trap. Carefully walk around me." Just as he said that, they heard a metallic clank where his foot was stuck.

"What was that?" asked Angelique, walking cautiously around him.

"A bear trap just sprang around my ankle."

A deafening rumbling sounded from their left side. From a fissure, a large millstone began rolling down toward François, who was pinned in place.

Chapter 9. Cat

Just as the policeman had said, flashing signs alerted motorists to possible traffic stoppages or slowdowns as we approached the city of Deva. Signs pointed to alternate routes.

"Well, Cat, there isn't any need to fight the traffic," said Tudor. "I'll take the highway to Hunedoara and bypass this mess. And we can visit the Corvin Castle after all."

I wondered why Angelique had told me to avoid this castle. Tapping my lips with my index finger, I remembered that this could be the castle where Vlad the Impaler and his nephew Vlad V had been imprisoned, and later, somewhere nearby in another underground dungeon, they had become infected and turned into vampires. This could be the castle where they returned as vampires, and scared King Corvinus to gladly let them go. Not to mention he even gave them an army to fight the Turks, the nemeses of Christian Europe.

"Tudor, what's the name of this castle again?"

"Corvin Castle," he answered.

That was a relief; it was not the same castle, or was it? "Where is Castelul de la Hunedoara?"

"It is the same castle."

"What? Are you sure?"

"Sure, I'm sure. It used to be called Castelul de la Hunedoara, or Hunyad Castle, but now it goes by Castelul Corvin—Corvin Castle. Why? Is there a problem?"

"Let me think." This was the castle I really wanted to see, but why did Angelique warn me not to? "Did Dracula ever visit this castle?"

"You tell me." He winked at me.

Of course—I was supposed to be the vampire expert. "I mean, are there historical records that Dracula was in this castle?"

"Yes, most likely."

Vlad V, my great-great-grandfather, and Vlad the Impaler, my great-great-granduncle, were held in or near this castle as prisoners, according to my great-great-grandfather. He told me that he had destroyed the tomb where he discovered the devil creature from which they had gotten infected and become vampires. Later he had built a church on top of the tomb. I looked around, wondering which church could that be. But there were many church spires in the distance.

As we continued on the highway, the Corvin Castle came into view. What a majestic castle it was, but frankly, not as scary as Bran Castle. What danger would be here in Corvin Castle? Danger such as we found in Sighisoara? I was worried, and I looked around, searching again for the church my great-grandfather built. It was futile. There were too many churches, and the city had grown since then. It might be located in an obscure part of the city of Hunedoara.

"You look worried, Cat," said Tudor. "This is not Sighisoara."

"I'm sure it's not," I said, trying to convince myself that everything was all right.

Tudor pulled into the parking lot in front of the castle, and we got out. It was an impressive castle, with a tall bridge across a deep ravine leading to the gates of the majestic, trapezoid-shaped tower with a red-tiled roof. To the left, another round tower reached for the sky, and crenellated medieval battlement walls surrounded it. To the right, the castle walls loomed high above the river that flowed underneath it, which served as an impassable moat. Four bay windows in the shape of small towers would have allowed their former occupants visibility over the domains below. It was a magical castle, and my curiosity to see it overtook my sense of caution.

"You should see inside," said Tudor, walking toward the bridge. I followed him. "For a long time, this castle was in ruins, just an empty shell. Then, a decade ago, a nonprofit organization paid millions of euros to refurbish the inside and restore it to its former glory from the time of King Corvinus."

"Is it a private castle like Bran Castle is?" I asked.

"No, it is a museum, although this nonprofit organization uses it for different activities after sundown."

"What?" I did a quick take. "It's used at night?"

"Yes, for meetings or parties. I have a friend who went to such a party. Or maybe it was a political rally or some benefit." He shrugged, unbothered by what he was saying.

I stopped and narrowed my eyes, suddenly seeing the castle in a different light. Bad vibes sounded alarms in my head. This castle was not what it seemed to be—a mere museum—but the home of a vampire organization.

"Tudor, we cannot go in there," I said, as I observed someone from one of the bay windows spying on us with binoculars.

"What's the matter, Cat?" He looked at my worried face as it drained of blood, but it was too late.

Four men with dark sunglasses surrounded us. I felt their cold vampire hands clutch at me. I turned to Tudor, who was held as well, and opened my mouth to scream. A sweet odor penetrated my nostrils, and I blacked out.

Chapter 10. Cat

I woke up in a canopy bed. Outside, I saw through the window that it was already night. Propping myself up on my elbows, I looked around and realized that I was in a medieval chamber of some kind. A candelabrum, standing on an ornate dark-walnut nightstand, illuminated the room with soft, flickering candles. Opposite the bed's footboard, a carved stone fireplace occupied most of the wall, and two high-backed chairs stood on either side of it. To my left, the leaded glass window was framed with sumptuous dark-blue velvet drapes, held open by gold, twisted ropes.

And then I looked at my attire. I was dressed in a long green silk dress, with ruffles around my décolletage. The sleeves reached my elbows and were trimmed with crocheted frills. I sat up, dumbfounded, wondering where I was and who had dressed me in this old-fashioned gown. I pulled my skirt up and underneath I found a white, ruffled petticoat. No wonder my hips looked huge! I turned over to get out of bed, but my ankles were bound with ropes attached to the bed's footboard.

There was no doubt—we had been taken captive in the castle's parking lot. But by whom? Who else? Queen Eleonore. I collapsed back into bed and began perspiring from the anxiety. Where was Tudor? I needed to talk to someone. I screamed at the top of my lungs, hoping to blast the window to pieces.

The heavy wooden door on my right creaked open, and a woman dressed as ridiculously as I was, except that her gown was light blue, came in. She had a pale complexion and wore a curly bee-hived, white wig. She was a vampire, and she sneered at me.

"Who are you? What's the meaning of this?" I demanded.

"No need to get all fussy, Catherina. You are the guest of our majesty, Queen Eleonore. My name is Lady Isolde."

I propped myself up on my elbows. "OK, Isolde. This charade is over. Untie me." I pointed to my feet. "And give me my clothes back."

She crossed her arms under her abundant breasts and stared at me. "Only the queen can order me to release you."

"Go and get her. Where is she?"

"Queen Eleonore is presently attending to other important matters."

I blew the hair off my face. "Who in the queen absence's can make decisions around here?"

"That would be Tristan, but he, too, is unavailable."

"Tristan and Isolde." I burst out laughing. "Is this a joke?"

"No, Catherina. This is very serious."

"OK, OK," I said. "Where is Dr. Tudor?"

"The doctor is resting, as should you."

"Is he in the next room?" I motioned with my head toward the door.

"No, he is detained in the dungeons."

"The what? The dungeons? Are you people mad? Who ordered for him to be thrown into the dungeons?"

"Our queen."

I collapsed back into the bed but then sat up. "Is there anyone here who can make an executive decision to untie me?"

"I'm afraid you must be kept in bed."

"I need to pee."

Isolde reached under my bed, pulled out a porcelain chamber pot, and placed it on my bed.

"You've got to be kidding me. I won't use that. Don't you have indoor plumbing? You may be a vampire from who knows when, but you must be aware of indoor plumbing," I said in a huffy voice.

"In the bed, in the pot, if you need to relieve yourself." She crossed her arms again, cocking her head.

"OK. Get out," I said while maneuvering myself to sit on the pot. "Can't you hear me? Get out!"

Very calmly she sat down on the chair near the door.

I needed to go, so I turned my back to her, reaching under ten pounds of skirt to remove my panties. Except that I had no panties on. They had removed even my underwear! That was the last straw. My Strigoi may not have any power against vampires, but I could still do some damage.

I pointed to the rope around my ankles and thought, *cut the rope*. I visualized the rope being cut. And just like that, the rope fell off my ankles.

I jumped off the bed, clenching one hand into a fist, while my other hand held the chamber pot high in the air, ready to create mayhem.

Isolde stood up, startled, and pointed at me. "You may have dark powers, but my queen prepared me for that possibility." She pulled a walkie-talkie from a side pocket and spoke into it: "Anubis, she's awake. Prepare to kill the doctor if she disobeys me." She looked at me with a raised eyebrow, daring me.

They had Tudor, and they would kill him if I summoned my Strigoi. I had no choice but to obey her for the time being. I sat on the bed, defeated.

"OK, I'll do as you say. Just get the hell out of this room."

"We have an understanding, then?" She nodded once and left me alone.

I pouted, and then I had to use the chamber pot.

Chapter 11. François and Angelique

The six-foot diameter, multi-ton millstone rolled as if on a track, straight toward François. He tried to pull his foot out of the trap, but the darn thing wouldn't budge. François stared at the stone rolling over to crush him. At first he took a stance as if to stop the stone, but it would have taken more than a vampire's strength to stop it. Rather than die, he decided to sacrifice his leg. He bent sideways to keep the stone from crushing him, but he knew his leg would be crushed.

With the stone a few feet from imminently obliterating his leg, a stalactite plunged down and jammed under the stone, making it jump off its guiding track. It missed François's leg by less than an inch. The stone slid down into the cave, crushing the calcium formations like twigs. Nearby, Angelique was dusting her hands.

"You threw that stalactite under the millstone," said François, relieved.

"A stalactite is a natural wedge," said Angelique. "The darn thing was harder to break than I thought."

"Thank you, Angelique. Without your help, I would have been a crippled vampire."

"Don't mention it. Let's get your foot out of that trap." She reached down and pushed the trap's latch release, and François pulled his leg out. Angelique inspected the trap below. "The trap is embedded in concrete. It was meant to catch a vampire, not a mere human."

"And to hold him down until the millstone rolled over him," concluded François. "This took a lot of planning and preparation."

"I wonder how many more traps await us?" Angelique looked around the cave, searching for any manmade—or, better yet, vampire-made—contraptions. "We'd better turn our head lamps on."

Vampires' eyes worked better in darkness than those of any other animal on Earth, although what they saw was grayish and grainy, and the details were not as easy to detect as they would be in full light. Given the situation, artificial light was needed.

François followed Angelique's recommendation and placed a headlamp on his forehead. He dusted off his pants leg, which was punctured in several places by the trap's teeth.

"How's your leg?" Angelique inquired.

"All healed." A vampire's blue blood had the characteristic of coagulating and instantly sealing most of a vampire body's wounds. Once the sharp, jagged edges of the trap had released their bite, the wounds on his calf healed in seconds. "I think we should stay off this path."

Angelique nodded. "I hope Mundibuto wasn't subjected to our bad surprise."

"Do you think Eleonore knows we're here?"

"I didn't detect anyone spying on us earlier," said Angelique. "But let's assume she knows we're here."

"Then we'd better be on guard." François pulled a magnum revolver with an ankle holster from his bag.

Angelique did the same, and she strapped the gun to her ankle. "Don't you think it would be easier to crawl on the cave's ceiling?" she wondered.

"You're right," agreed François.

Both of them hoisted the bags onto their backs and, as agile as cats, they climbed the cave's walls to the ceiling, where they continued on all fours, crawling upside down. Creeping on the ceiling was slower than walking on the bumpy ground of the cave, but it was safer, in case other traps had been planted on the path.

They stopped on a ledge to assess which way to go next. In front of them, a large chamber opened up, forested with dozens of hanging stalactites. Down below, water cascaded into the steeply descending chute. Below, the underground river seemed to drain as if through the hole of a funnel.

"What do you think, Angelique? Should we swing from stalactite to stalactite to cross to the other side?"

"It'd be better than walking on the loose and slippery stones." With her flashlight, Angelique inspected the underground canyon, until she found what she was looking for. "The trail on which the zombies entered or exited is over there. There are lots of places in which to set traps for the unsuspecting."

"Stalactites it is, then." François jumped thirty feet across and latched onto a drapery stalactite.

Angelique leaped and clung to a thick stalactite nearby. Methodically, she climbed up to its base, from where she jumped to the next stalactite. François followed her, sometimes using the same stalactite she did. Jumping from stalactite to stalactite was faster than crawling on the ceiling, and in no time they were closer to where the wall of the cave plunged down hundreds of feet to where the river drained. Ahead of them, one last row of stalactites, resembling an upside-down picket fence, awaited their leaps.

"Those stalactites look like teeth," said François.

Angelique laughed. "Yes, I feel as if I am just about to jump into the throat of a giant monster, right through its teeth." She eyed which stalactite would be the best to jump to. "Some of them are dry."

"Good. They're safer to grab," said François.

Both of them jumped simultaneously, aiming for two dry stalactites, one next to the other. They grabbed one each, but the columns of limestone cracked and broke as if they were made of plaster. Angelique and François did not have time to even make a sound as they plunged down to their deaths.

Chapter 12. Mundibuto

Mundibuto walked around the narrow stone cell, climbing over the stalactite in the middle of the floor, checking for weaknesses. The walls were limestone; the two end caps were granite. He placed his ear on the wall that was closest to the stream and heard the water trickling beyond. He thought that, depending on the thickness of that wall, he might be able to break through using the geologist's hammer in his bag. But it would take time. The granite end caps, after he examined them in more detail, seemed to have closed by swinging down. Each might have rotated on a pinion at the top of the ceiling. Using the geologist's hammer, he tapped on the walls, listening for variations in thickness. No hollow sound resonated from any place he tapped, including the wall through which the sound of the water could be heard. Each wall was solid.

Sitting down he analyzed the situation. After this first inspection, it looked bleak. He was hopelessly trapped in a stone cell. In a few hours, the queen would have discovered the disaster he and Cat had left behind in Sighisoara, and she would surely come back and kill him.

A thought occurred to him: She had mentioned that she would drown him. Why drown him, when there were so many other methods of killing him available to her? But maybe, trapped in here, there were only two ways to die: by starvation or by drowning.

Drowning him would require thousands of gallons of water. The underground creek he had walked along before didn't have much flow, and it would take days to fill his chamber. But maybe there was a reservoir of water somewhere upstream, which could flood his cell quickly. Once flooded, Mundibuto would last only hours underwater. Still, why flood it just to drown someone trapped inside, even a vampire? The end caps attracted his attention again, and he started to inspect them once more, this time more diligently.

Gravity kept both end caps closed. They must be held open by some mechanism or by simple stops that, when pulled, would force the slabs down and close the chamber. Each end cap must weigh many tons. How could these slabs be lifted to open the chamber? Hydraulic pressure was one answer. Water held in storage somewhere would provide the needed pressure to lift the end caps. Flooding the chamber might be necessary to open it, and the same water would drown him. The mechanism worked through buoyancy? A flotation mechanism would be easier to build.

Mundibuto inspected the walls for any holes through which the water could get in, but he found none. The walls were smooth and solid except for the niche that Eleonore had used. Could the water come in through there?

Or…

Mundibuto stared at the gravel floor. The water could percolate up through the gravel, flooding the chamber and raising the end caps.

Not wanting to waste any more time speculating, he used his large hands to dig through the gravel near the upstream cap down to the solid floor beneath. He found only solid limestone.

He had hoped to find some kind of flotation container underneath the stone gate. Instead, the stone slab was tightly embedded in a groove in the floor. He remembered the way the passageway had dropped down and then up again as he entered this chamber. That's where the two gates came down in. With his back to the stone, he slid down to the ground, disillusioned by his efforts to find a way out.

Judging by the width of the trench he had crossed coming in here, the slab-gate was four feet thick. How could he escape? The stalactite that had crushed the skeleton and triggered the closing of the end caps stood in the middle of the floor, implanted in the gravel bed. It had taken that much weight to unlatch the opening mechanism. What was underneath the point of impact?

Quickly he cleared the pebbles from around it. To his delight, he found the trigger underneath. The stalactite's tip was resting on a round stone. After he clear more gravel, he reached the limestone bottom. The trigger, the round stone the stalactite had hit, was a hefty column that was depressed into the floor. There had to be a cavity underneath it. He pushed the stalactite off the trigger and cleared the remaining pieces of gravel left around the stone column.

Mundibuto pulled and pushed on the column and, after the sand around the bottom cleared around the perimeter he could move the column back and forth. It was possible that the hole the column had plugged was his access to freedom. The trigger did not lift up after he pushed the stalactite off, therefore, he reasoned, the column was resting on some lever that was not spring loaded. He needed to lift the column up. Fortunately, the top of the column had a lip. He clenched his fingers around the lip and, using his legs, he slowly pulled the column out. After it cleared the hole, he threw it aside and peered down into the hole. Below, he saw a copper beam that must have been the lever that had disengaged the latches. The unplugged hole was roughly one foot in diameter. A cavity of about three feet opened up beneath the copper beam.

Besides strength and quickness, flexibility was another of the many capabilities that a vampire possessed. A vampire could pass through openings smaller than the largest section of his body, dislocating and realigning his bones and molding his muscles to fit through even a 12-inch round hole. Mundibuto was able to go through it in spite of the fact that his shoulders were 24 inches across. After passing his bag through the hole, slowly and methodically, head first, he began squeezing through.

Half an hour later he was in the cavity below.

Chapter 13. Cat

After using the disgusting chamber pot, I began pacing the room, unsure of what to do next. It was obvious that Eleonore, the self-crowned queen of the vampires, had kidnapped me to lure my friends Mundibuto, Angelique, and François to surrender. And what if they surrendered? What would she do next? Subjugate them, even kill them? What about Tudor's fate, and mine? I was less concerned about me than about Tudor. He was a mere mortal and expendable. I was a mortal, too, but I was Vlad V's great-granddaughter. I had status, or so I hoped. Vampire society would not take lightly such a transgression against me. But then, considering that I knew only three vampires well, I wasn't so sure.

What would Eleonore do when she found out that Mundibuto and I had destroyed her army of zombies and proto-vampires? What kind of revenge would the queen take on Mundibuto and me? I shuddered, not seeing anything good coming out of this, feeling helpless.

Sure, I had my ghostly guardians, the Strigoi, but they could only protect me, not take action against vampires. My Strigoi weren't of any use as long as Eleonore had Tudor. I couldn't move a finger without jeopardizing his life, but I needed to see him, to see if he was all right and unharmed.

Someone unlocked the door, and Isolde came in. She was talking on a cell phone. "Yes, your majesty." She pulled the phone from her ear. "The queen would like to talk to you." She extended her arm to hand me the phone.

Queen, my ass, I thought. Instead, I decided to be civilized. I took the phone and said, "What's the meaning of this, Eleonore?"

"Now, now. That is not the proper manner in which to speak to a queen, is it?" Her voice was high and whiny, and she was trying to come across as an accommodating royal.

"Why did you kidnap Dr. Lupu and me?"

"For your own protection, my dear." She spoke with a German accent.

"What protection? Who are you pretending to protect us from?"

"Three very unruly vampires who want your head. I believe you've met them—Vlady, Nicolae, and Ilie."

Nicolae and Ilie I knew; they'd lost *their* heads instead. But who was Vlady? Probably the one I had called Fakeula. "If they are in your employment, why don't you tell them to stand down?" I hoped she understood the military jargon.

"They are my subjects, not my employees. I haven't heard from them in a week, and I'm afraid for your safety. Eager as they are to please me, they may harm you and you need protection. I want to assure you that you are safe in my palace."

"Thanks, but I'd feel a lot safer if you'd let Dr. Lupu and me go."

"Not until I hear from them." Her voice was steely now.

Considering that the three of them were dead and that I had had a big part in killing them, she wasn't going to hear from them. "I don't care if you hear from them. What you've done, by abducting Dr. Lupu and me, is criminal. I'm going to report you to the police."

"The police," she giggled. "The police work for me, dear. Just like the officer who found you two screwing in the car on the side of the road. He advised you to take the detour, which you did. And you came to my palace. For protection."

I felt like a marionette. She was pulling my strings, and I had to do as she commanded. The good thing, at least for now, was that she didn't know about her subjects being dead and her army being turned to sand. Why didn't she know that yet? Maybe that's why Tudor and I were able to enjoy a mini-vacation and why she hadn't abducted us before. I should have left Transylvania when I had the chance.

"Very well, then," I said in a conciliatory tone. "Since we are under your *protection*, I expect to be treated like a guest, not a prisoner. Please release Dr. Lupu."

"Of course, you'll be treated like an honored guest. However, the dear doctor has to remain sequestered in order for you to behave."

"Behave? What do you mean?" I played dumb.

"I know that you've inherited the Strigoi from Vlad. And you even used them in my palace to cut the rope that tied you to the footboard. Isolde warned you that if you don't obey us, Dr. Lupu would suffer the consequences." She paused for impact. "Did I make myself clear?"

She had me. I had no choice but to pretend that I'd obey. "Understood. How do you know about my Strigoi?"

"Oh, dear. Vlad and I go back a long time, and I saw him using them against mortals and vampires alike. I figured that he gave them to you, although you are a mortal."

"Hmm," I said, stumped to say anything else.

"Hmm, it is," she said. "You command the Strigoi, but since you are a mere human, you cannot command them to harm us vampires. You'd better obey if you want Dr. Lupu to remain unharmed."

Chapter 14. Cat

I handed the phone back to Isolde, who, without saying a word to me, left the room while chatting on the phone with her queen.

I was fuming over the situation at hand. I felt trapped. I had to do something. I headed for the door, except that I tripped on the hem of my long dress and fell flat on my face. Curses flooded my mind, but I decided to stay calm. I untangled myself from my clothes and got up. The garb I was dressed in was not conducive to quick action, but somehow I had to improvise. I picked up one side and then the other of my skirt and petticoat and shoved them under the satin belt at my waist. At least now I could walk without using my hands to constantly pull the skirt up.

Satisfied with my makeshift skirt and ignoring my lack of undies, I walked to the door and grabbed the handle to open it. Damn Isolde, she'd locked me in the room. I would show her what it means to keep me bolted inside. Calling for my Strigoi, I concentrated and imagined the heavy wooden door blowing outward in a zillion splinters. Instead, the whole door flew out, intact with its doorjamb and hinges, across the hall, propping itself up against the wall. That would do; that was good enough.

First, I stuck my head out through the opening to search the hallway. I looked left, and it was all clear. I looked right, and it was all clear. Then I saw a shadow descend on me. I screamed and raised my arms for protection. The darn door I had just blown out fell down toward me and would have crushed me if my Strigoi hadn't stopped it. The door stopped a few inches above me. I motioned to the right with my hands to shove the door aside and it became airborne, crashing against a door at the end of the hallway.

At least now I was free. Where should I start looking, to the left or the right? It didn't matter, so I turned left, sprinting down the corridor just to hurtle smack into Isolde and another pompous lady-in-waiting. They stood their ground. I was flat on my back.

Isolde placed her hands on her hips, frowning. "I told you to stay in your room until the queen returns."

They towered over me. The other lady, much taller and beefier than Isolde, crossed her arms and jutted her chin out as if reaffirming the order. I grabbed my knees and stood up, and for a moment I felt like a little girl caught by the teacher and the principal skipping class.

But I shook off that feeling. "I want to see Dr. Lupu," I said in an imperial tone. That seemed to have worked because both vampires stared at each other in disbelief. I wasn't sure if they were impressed by my tone or my audacity. "Now!" I yelled.

Isolde reached for her walkie-talkie. I motioned with my hand, and the walkie-talkie flew from her hand into mine, thanks to my Strigoi. Her mouth gaped in surprise. The other vampire lady seemed to be taken aback as well. She retracted her chin and her eyes widened, especially when she saw the smashed door at the other end of the hallway. What I'd done was far and above what a vampire would expect.

"I'll speak slowly and use small words so you can understand me," I said, narrowing my eyes. "If anything happens to Dr. Lupu, I'll tear this castle down with you in it.

You take me to see him right now, and he'd better not be hurt. Understood?"

They both nodded, unsure of what I might do next. They were vampires and I was just a human, but I possessed dark powers that they did not have or understand.

"Let's go." I motioned with the walkie-talkie.

We descended on wide marble steps to the first level of the castle, and then we took a narrower set of stone stairs down to the basement. Occasionally, an oil lamp would light our passage. Isolde and the big vampire lady were leading, and occasionally one or the other looked over her shoulder at me apprehensively. We kept descending and, from what I could figure, we had gone down another level to the dungeons. It was humid down there and it smelled like mildew and rot. I saw some rats darting around, and I tried hard not to flinch.

We stopped in front of a rough-cut wooden door with black iron hinges and rivets. The big lady pounded on it. A small viewer-window opened and someone looked out at us from behind the door.

"Let us in, Anubis," said Isolde.

The answer that came back was not in words but in canine squeals.

"I know what the orders are, but she's going berserk," replied Isolde, motioning to me.

The vampire, or whatever he was, unlocked the door and opened it inward slowly, while the door's rusty hinges squeaked. What stepped outside made my heart skip more than one beat. The creature was humanoid but had the head of an animal, a jackal.

Chapter 15. Cat

The creature standing in the doorway was a muscular, bare-chested man with a head of a jackal. It had to be a mask. His only clothing was a dirty loincloth around his waist, and he wore leather sandals. His black eyes looked at me intently. His head and neck were covered in black and dark-brown fur, and his snout wrinkled from time to time. That was some good mask.

"What in God's creation are you?" I managed to ask.

"Anubis," he replied in an understandable human tongue.

Anubis? The Egyptian god with a human body and the head of a jackal, who ushers dead souls into the underworld? Was this guy a vampire, and did he wear a mask for kicks? I had to ask, "Anubis, are you a vampire?"

He nodded his jackal head.

"Why are you wearing that mask?"

He shook his head. "Not mask. My head." His large ears moved as if to tune into other sounds.

"Where do you come from? I mean, how did you get that head?"

"Our queen made me this way."

"Queen Eleonore von Schwarzenberg?"

He nodded and made a small, lamenting squeal.

The creature in front of me looked like a figure out of an Egyptian tomb. From what he said, he once was a man, or a vampire, and the queen changed him. I'd have to find out the details later, because at that moment I wanted to see Tudor.

"Where is Dr. Lupu?"

Anubis shook his head. "Not allowed."

Another nonbeliever, so it was time to impress him. I lifted my hand, pointed it at the door he'd just opened, and commanded, "Sawdust."

In an instant, the door collapsed in a pile of sawdust, with the black hardware sticking out of the small mound. Only the two heavy hinges were left hanging from the doorjamb. The two vampire women stepped back, covering their mouths in fear. Anubis looked at the heap of dust and, without saying a word, motioned to me to follow him inside the vaulted brick, low-ceilinged room, which had rows of iron-barred cells along two walls. The only illumination came from the outside oil lamps.

I found Tudor in the second cell, curled up on the floor in a fetal position.

"What did you do to him?" I turned to Anubis, ready to tear him apart.

"I threw him in there. Locked him up."

Apparently Tudor hadn't awakened from the drug they'd given us when we were kidnapped. I kneeled down and reached through the bars to stroke his hair. He stirred and slowly opened his eyes.

"Tudor, are you OK?"

"Cat, are you all right?"

"I'm fine. How do you feel?"

"Groggy. Thirsty." He sat up and looked at me. "Why are you dressed like that?"

"Period garb. Compliments of the queen." I looked at Anubis and said, "Let him out."

Anubis stood there, unsure of what to do.

The big woman vampire got closer and said, "Don't you dare let him out."

I stood up. It was time to teach this vampire-broad who was in charge. "Hey, babe. What's your name?"

She looked down at me with her hands on her hips. "Lady Ladeena." And then, quicker than a snake, she grabbed me by the throat. That wasn't good. Her large hand and long fingers almost wrapped around my neck. She lifted me slightly until I was on my tiptoes.

I was caught. Being held by her or any other vampire did me little good—I couldn't use my Strigoi to escape. "Let me go," I managed to say.

"Not a chance. You cannot do anything against me while I have you by the throat." She barked at Anubis, "You were supposed to put the man in shackles!"

Anubis gestured as if to say, "What for?"

"Damn you!" she screamed at him. "Put a rope around the doctor's neck, tie it to the hook on the ceiling, put him on a stool, and if this bitch gives us any more problems, kick the stool out from under him."

Anubis efficiently did as he was told. First, he tied Tudor's hands behind his back. Then he tied a rope with a noose to the iron hook on the vaulted ceiling, stood Tudor on a stool, and placed the noose around his neck.

"Tie a pull cord to the stool," ordered Ladeena, while still holding me by my throat.

Anubis tied a rope to the stool and pulled it outside the cell, after which he locked the gate. Just a yank of the rope and Tudor would hang. And I was still being held by my throat.

Ladeena dragged me to the last cell down the hallway and threw me onto the muddy floor. She snapped her fingers. Anubis came quickly and locked the cell's iron-barred door with a heavy key.

"You've been told—if you value your friend's life, don't make a move," Ladeena pointed her finger at me.

I sat on the muddy floor, boiling with rage, but they had Tudor with a noose around his neck.

Chapter 16. Mundibuto

Mundibuto crawled upstream along the corroded-green copper shaft and exited beyond the slab-gate that had entrapped him. He was free, and he vowed that he would not be caught in a trap again. Or at least not in the same trap. However, he had to know how this contraption worked in case he needed that knowledge in the future. He ran the beam of his flashlight along the stone slab-gate and, as he had speculated, he found above it an enormous oak barrel—no, not even enormous; "humongous" was a better way to describe the size of the oak barrel encased in green copper rings. That was what would serve as the flotation device that would eventually raise the slabs in the open position when the entire underground chamber was flooded.

He climbed higher in the cave along the creek and came across an underground lake. The creek was draining into it from upstream, and at his end it trickled out through the cracks of a large flap gate made of stone. That was the valve that, once opened, would flood the chambers below and open the two stone slab gates that had trapped him. Ingenious, he thought.

To continue to wherever this trail led, he would have to swim across the reservoir-lake, or...why not walk? After a quick inspection, he found the lever that opened the flap gate. First, he made sure that if he opened it he would be safe. Then he kicked the copper lever. It didn't take much force. The flap valve opened, allowing a deluge of water to flood the cave below. The water rose up to the giant barrel and slowly lifted it, creaking as it went up. That in turn raised the stone gate below, until it locked in an open position. The stone cell was flooded with water and soon the other stone gate opened, draining the water out of the cell he was previously trapped in.

Stone against stone boomed, and he saw the flap valve close and dam the reservoir-lake again for the next cycle. He smiled, satisfied that now there was no longer a lake but just a creek filling it up again. His job was finished there, so he proceeded cautiously upstream.

It was eight a.m., although it made no difference in the cave. Mundibuto wondered if François and Angelique had fared better and had been able to reach their destination. According to his altimeter, he had climbed several hundred meters inside the mountain. The cave his friends had entered was most likely descending, and he expected to find them somewhere along the trail or to meet them at whatever underground compound Eleonore had built for her nefarious reasons.

At the end of the now dry reservoir, the creek cascaded down from above in a column of water through a vertical shaft, which had spiraling stone steps along its walls. To make sure that he was on the right track, he turned on the yellow light and found traces of indigo hue circling the shaft's walls. That was the path, but…such a path could easily contain a missing or collapsing step, and he could fall. This time he would do it his way, so he climbed along the walls of the shaft, avoiding the stairs. On two occasions, he found several places on the spiraling stairs that were intended to cause the sudden fall of the unaware.

He reached the top and climbed up into a small chamber. The creek flowed in from a tunnel, which was chiseled out of the creek's original waterway to enlarge the passage. Mundibuto stooped, half-bent, to walk through the tunnel.

It reminded him that this could be another trap. He shone his light at the mouth of the shaft he had climbed up through and discovered another trap. A flat, large stone stood on its end, right over the mouth of the shaft. He walked carefully behind the stone and found the copper levers that would release the flat stone so it would fall and cap the shaft he'd just climbed out of. This trap was behind him now and not a danger.

The queen was either paranoid or meticulous about keeping her secrets. What else was ahead? He was certain that this was not the last trap. But there was the tunnel, narrow, chiseled out of solid rock, and potentially dangerous. He sat down crossed legged at the entrance of the tunnel to consider his next move. He wondered why there were so many rather sophisticated traps in here. Was the queen trying to keep humans, or vampires, out? Definitely vampires. She had planned for this a long time ago, and she knew that the time would come when she'd be facing the wrath of some of the vampires, like Vlad V and his friends.

He looked inside the tunnel, thinking. A human could walk through it half-bent, and triggers would be positioned on the creek's bed. A vampire could walk like a human or crawl on the ceiling, so additional triggers might be located on the ceiling as well. The only way that remained to get through the tunnel—and hopefully Eleonore hadn't considered it—was to crawl horizontally halfway up the curved walls of the tunnel. Having made the decision, he moved into the tunnel, carefully checking that the mouth of the tunnel had not been booby-trapped. There were two spots that seemed suspect. Bypassing them, he entered the tunnel, propping himself up on one wall with his legs and on the opposite wall with his arms. Slowly and meticulously, facing down, he advanced in a horizontal position that no human would have been able to maintain for more than a few yards, if at all. Midway, the tunnel bent to the right, and he took great care not to touch the corners. Soon after that, another bend turned straight up, which he crawled cautiously to the top.

His head popped out of the tunnel-turned-shaft, and he spied nearby a large stone ball on an inclined trough, waiting patiently to be unlatched and to roll down to plug the shaft. He was pleased with his progress, but he didn't let his guard down. He jumped out of the shaft without touching its rim. He stood up in another small cave, ornate with stalactites and stalagmites, and with several passage openings to other caves. The access that attracted his attention was straight ahead. It was another anti-vampire passageway, in a triangular shape about 10 feet high and wide.

He turned his yellow tracer light on and saw the trail going into the triangular opening of the tunnel. Another trail connected from his right up a naturally made access shaft. There were traces of zombies in that shaft as well. But the triangular passageway was where he probably needed to go, which presented a risky route. Mundibuto was sure that the multiple cracks in the floor were pressure-plate triggers, but he could not crawl horizontally on the angled walls of the triangular passage as he had before. The walls were finely polished, offering nothing to grip on. His only alternative was to step cautiously on what seemed to be solid ground and not on the parts that might collapse under his feet.

Slowly and carefully, he advanced on all fours, stepping carefully to avoid any trigger plate, although the floor had so many cracks that the whole floor might have been made of such triggers. When he was about halfway through, the stone floor suddenly opened up, and he fell in. The passage's floor closed just as quickly above him.

He landed in total darkness on the rough floor of a cavernous chamber littered with human bones.

Chapter 17. François and Angelique

Angelique's stalactite broke and fell first, but in that split of a second, François assessed the ground below before his stalactite crumbled as well. He plunged headfirst and caught Angelique, who was still scrambling from the surprise of her fall. She instinctively knew that François had a plan for their unwanted fall and she relaxed, aligning her body with his. Both dived down, arms spread like eagles' wings, into the deep and dark chasm below.

The cave floor below was thick with spearing stalagmites that made a deadly landing spot, even for vampires, if the impact didn't kill them first. François aimed for the black hole where the underground river drained. He hoped that they had enough height to glide several feet forward and land in that watery hole below. Just moments before impact, François rotated Angelique and himself, so they could land feet first.

Down below, as the water squeezed out through a drain hole, it formed a body of water that François hoped would be deep enough to soften their landing. They landed in the water, but not exactly in the center where the hole was. They hit the water with a big splash and their butts slid along the funnel's wall, scraping the rocky sides all the way to the drain hole, where they fell through a column of water down into an underground pool. Their impact caused a splash that almost emptied the pool they splashed in. They were bruised and battered, but alive. They took a few minutes to lie in the water to let their bodies recover and heal. It was a fall that would have killed any human, and although it didn't kill the two vampires, it was unpleasant—even downright painful.

Angelique was the first to recover, having been lucky enough to fall on top of François when they landed in the funnel above. She sat up in the shallow water. "Fuck!" She shouted and swiped the water off her face.

François slowly floated on his back to the shore and then turned over on his belly. Soon he felt better, and he crawled out of the water and sat on the stony shore with his head between his knees, letting the water drip from his hair.

"Are you OK, Angelique?" he asked after a while.

"Yes, how about you?"

"I'm well, or as well as I can be after that damn fall." He twisted his neck, which gave a loud crack.

Angelique crawled out of the water and sat next to him, placing an arm around his shoulders. "Thank you, François. Without you, I would have been a dead vampire—broken to pieces."

"Don't mention it." He smoothed his hair with his hands. "Who would have thought to plant fake stalactites on the ceiling?"

"Someone who expected vampires would crawl on the ceiling of the cave."

"This is one evil woman."

"And a vampire," added Angelique. "I hope Mundibuto had an easier time."

François lay back to recover some more, while Angelique gingerly got to her feet. The pool that had cushioned their final fall refilled quickly, and it continued to flow down a stone crevasse. Angelique removed her smashed headlamp and discarded it. She reached in her bag that was floating nearby and removed a flashlight, after which she walked to the mouth of the underground stream and inspected the path below.

"It seems to be an easy descent. I wonder how much farther?"

François consulted his wrist altimeter, which surprisingly had survived, just like his headlamp. "We entered the cave about 1,000 meters above the valley floor at Rasnov. We've descended 600 meters so far, and we came down almost another 200 meters in that last fall. I'm sure we'll meet Mundibuto somewhere soon. Maybe another 100 meters or so down." He stood up stiffly.

It took them another hour to fully recover from the fall and feel like themselves again. As soon as they were well and dry enough, they picked up their packs and began descending along the trickling underground river, being twice as cautious as before.

Minutes later, both of them assessed the strange triangular opening leading down the path to their mysterious destination.

"What do you think?" François asked Angelique.

"The floor has so many cracks that must contain triggers for something nasty to follow."

"Yes, and we cannot use the walls to traverse this triangular tunnel. They are polished smooth."

"Everything is vampire-made and vampire-proof here," Angelique said, looking around. "Even that big round ball."

"That's another trap—it's meant to cap the mouth of that hole when triggered." François pointed to the hole from where Mundibuto had earlier exited.

Angelique squatted down and turned her flashlight on, inspecting the coarse sand on the floor around the rim of the hole. "Footprints. These are large. Maybe Mundibuto's?"

François bent down and checked the prints, and he followed them to the triangular entrance. "He went in. I hope he came out at the other end." He pulled out a pair of binoculars and looked down the path. "The floor is stony at the other end. Hard to say if he made it."

Angelique cupped her hands around her mouth and called, "Mundibuto!" A slight echo bounced around, but no other reply came back.

"Maybe he is deep on the other side," speculated François. "Follow me and step on my foot steps."

Angelique made a gesture as if to say, I wish we didn't have to do this.

François stepped in, half-crouched, while inspecting for deep cracks that might give up the location of a trigger plate. Occasionally, he blew the sand out of the cracks to make sure it was safe. Angelique followed him a few yards back, stepping cautiously where he placed his feet. The advance was slow, but there were no surprises until François reached the middle.

The floor opened up under François and swallowed him in an instant.

Quickly, Angelique grabbed onto the cracks of the floor with her fingers and somehow managed to find enough grip not to tumble down after him.

Chapter 18. The Vampires

François felt the ground open up so quickly that he didn't have time to react. On his way down he kept his eyes on the opening above him, but it closed before he could land and jump up and out of the hole he'd fallen into. He landed amid a pile of human bones, crushing many into smaller pieces like twigs.

"I beat you to it," a voice boomed in the dark.

"Mundibuto! There you are. I was wondering if you had fared any better."

"No, just like you, I fell in." Mundibuto gave François a friendly but manly embrace. "Where is Angelique?"

"She's up there." François pointed up. "Wisely, we went in one at a time, and she didn't fall in."

"Angelique!" shouted Mundibuto, staring upward.

Both of them perked their ears to hear a response, but they could only hear their breathing.

"Did you hear Angelique when she called for you earlier?" Francois asked.

"No, nothing. This place is quiet as a tomb."

"Did you try to get out through the ceiling?"

"Yes, I tried. The ceiling is smooth as glass. I couldn't crawl underneath it," Mundibuto sighed.

"At least you made it this far," said François.

"I have some stories to tell you. Did you and Angelique encounter any traps?"

"Many. This place was made to prevent vampires from getting in." François stared at the skulls and bones on the ground. "Whose are these?"

"They're all human," answered Mundibuto.

"How did they make it so far in?"

"I don't think they came in," said Mundibuto. "They were trying to get out."

"That makes sense—they were victims of the queen."

"Whom I've just met," said Mundibuto.

"What? Where?"

"In a trap I was caught in. She was attending a Haydn concert in the cave near the Rasnov fortress. She looked in on me after I was trapped."

"Why didn't you grab her by the throat?"

"I tried to, but I only caught her wig."

"How did she seem?"

"I've never met her before, but she seemed to be one evil creature."

"She hasn't changed. Brace yourself for more pleasantries," François said sarcastically.

"You've met her?"

"Once or twice." François looked up. "I wonder how Angelique is doing up there."

Angelique backpedaled from the middle of the corridor. The floor had opened so fast that François had no chance to save himself. And then it closed just as fast.

She called, "François! François!" There was no response, other than the sound of her voice bouncing off the hard rock. She feared that the opening below may be a deep one and that François was too far down and perhaps hurt.

Angelique retraced her steps and exited the triangular corridor. She paced around, thinking how she could come to François's rescue. She had no rope in her bag, so even if she managed to open the trap, he would have to climb out on his own. She had to find a way to open the trap and keep it open. She turned around, looking for something to use as a tool or brace, but there was nothing but small rocks and some small stalactites and stalagmites. Nothing sizable enough to stick in the gap when she would trigger the opening of the floor, except...

The big, stone ball stood silently nearby, ready to roll and cap the nearby hole in the floor. The stone was almost six feet in diameter and must have weighed 10 tons or more, she figured. A chiseled, tapered stone wedge acted as a stop under the ball. When triggered, that wedge would retract and the stone would roll along a trough and plug the hole in the floor. What she needed to do was to get the ball rolling into the triangular passage.

The problem was that the guiding stone trough was severely inclined toward the hole, and diverting it from that path to the triangular passage would be tricky. If she did manage to get the ball rolling the way she wanted, her job would be easier afterward, as the floor to the triangular passage was tilting toward its center. Gravity would nudge the ball, which would either collapse the stone floor or jam the trapdoor open. The important task was to make the ball roll where she wanted it, and although she was powerful, she was not powerful enough to dislodge a 10-ton stone off its cradle.

Angelique searched her bag for tools she might use and she found, to her surprise, two bars of plastic explosives and accessories. It was very thoughtful of Mundibuto to include such a delightful accessory, she thought. Quickly she molded the two bars to the contour of the cradle's stone lip facing the triangular opening, and then she inserted the blast caps. The ball was ready to roll. But in case the ball needed additional persuasion to follow the right path, she broke a stalactite from the ceiling and shoved it into the trough under the ball in front of the wedge.

She moved back a safe distance, said a quick prayer—she believed in God—and pushed the button on the remote control of the detonator. A loud explosion disintegrated the stone lip under the rock ball, but the round stone just stood there. Then, a moment later, the ball started moving lazily out of its cradle. Angelique jumped for joy, seeing the ball heading for the triangular mouth of the passage.

Except that the ball got stuck, being slightly larger than the triangular opening. Not only didn't she manage to get the ball in but now it was blocking the entrance to the forsaken passage.

Chapter 19. Cat

I stood up and grabbed the bars of my cell, like any prisoner would. I held on to them and called out loudly, "Tudor, are you OK?"

"As well as I can be," he said in a scratchy voice. The noose was probably too tight around his neck.

I propped my forehead against the bars. Yes, I could blast the bars to smithereens, but I couldn't touch Anubis because he would pull the stool out from under Tudor. I was cornered, I was neutralized, and I had to wait in that miserable place as the mud squeezed up between my toes. I sighed, depressed by our situation. And the worst hasn't even started yet. The repercussions of our acts in Sighisoara made me shiver with fear.

Could my vampire friends help me? Maybe, if they got here before the queen arrived. But they had no idea where I was, or what predicament I was in together with Tudor. I touched my cross pendant, which had a mini-transmitter in it, and once it saved my life, alerting François of my location. But, the transmitter may not have enough range and François and my friends may not monitor the signal.

For sure, Eleonore would use me to counter my friends. I couldn't see a way out of this, except for...

Except for the ampule with the vampire blue blood that was inserted behind my right ear. Before Vlad died, he gave me a drop of his blue blood, contained in a small diamond ampule, which François inserted surgically under the skin behind my ear. In case I wanted to become a vampire, or if I was in big trouble—as I was now—I could open the ampule by squeezing it under my skin, and I would become infected with vampire blood. According to Vlad, I would effectively turn into a vampire within seconds. He didn't say how quickly and how much of a vampire I would become, and if I would be as strong and quick as the other vampires, although I imagined that it would take time for me to develop into a full vampire like Angelique, no matter how quickly the blue blood worked. Nevertheless, he insisted that as soon as the blue blood entered my bloodstream, I would be able to defend myself.

I'd encountered deadly situations before, but I had resisted becoming a vampire, and somehow I had prevailed. I had even saved Angelique from being sold by the Goth cult to Dr. Hellinherr. But at that time, I was dealing with mere mortals. Now I was dealing with vampires, and one of them had the head of a jackal.

But wait—I had to give myself some credit. In Sighisoara, I killed two of Eleonore's vampires. Sure, I had help from Mundibuto and Tudor, but I was victorious. At this moment, however, I wasn't feeling that victorious. I had encountered eight vampires so far: four in the parking lot when we were abducted, the queen, Isolde, Ladeena, and Anubis. I had a feeling there were more of them.

"Anubis!" I called to the jackal-headed vampire. I couldn't see him or Tudor as I was in a cell on the same side of Tudor's cell. "Anubis, answer me!"

"Not allowed," he answered reluctantly.

"Who doesn't allow you to talk to me?"

"Isolde. Ladeena."

"I don't remember them telling you that. Come on, you can talk to the great-granddaughter of Vlad the Fifth."

I heard him sighing.

"How did you become Anubis?"

"The queen made me."

"She made you? How could she do that? Why?"

"To punish me."

"What did you do to deserve such a transfiguration?"

"Insubordination."

"Were you a vampire when she changed you?"

"Yes."

"How long ago was that?"

"Fifty-some years ago."

"And how long have you been a vampire?"

"A century and a half."

"Are you happy to be Anubis?"

There was a moment of silence. "No."

"Will the queen change you back?"

"Maybe, now that Vlad the Fifth is dead."

The plot thickens, I thought. "What does Vlad have to do with you being transformed?"

"Long story."

"You can tell me. I'm Catherina, Vlad's great-granddaughter." I wanted to make sure he understood whom he was talking to.

"Yes, you are, but you're not him. You're not even a vampire."

Something worth knowing had happened in the past between Eleonore and Vlad. "Were other vampires punished like you?"

"Yes. One more."

"Who's that? What happened?"

"He was my friend and he, too, was insubordinate. She punished both of us."

"What did she turn him into?"

"He has the head of a falcon. His name is Ra."

"Ra? You mean the Egyptian sun god?"

"Only in his image."

This sounded monstrous. It was bad enough to be a vampire, but to look like a freak was another thing. What kind of dark soul would do that to another being?

"Anubis, I met a vampire who resembled Vlad. Do you know him?"

"That is Vlady, the queen's lover. She transformed him to look like Vlad the Fifth."

Holy crap! I felt my hair standing up on end from fear. What had I just done in Sighisoara? I had killed Vlady, Eleonore's lover. When she finds out who killed him, she's going to tear me limb from limb.

Chapter 20. Cat

"Anubis, did Fakeula—I mean—Vlady always look like Vlad?"

"No, she made him that way."

"When?"

"About 40 years ago."

That was when Vlad began aging. There must have been something going on between Eleonore and Vlad.

"Was Vlady happy to look like Vlad?"

"He was willing to be transformed."

Tudor made a gagging sound.

"Anubis, would you loosen the noose from around Dr. Lupu's neck?"

"Why?"

"He is uncomfortable, and if God forbid something happens to him, all hell will break loose."

"You cannot harm me."

"Oh yes, I can. You may be a vampire, but you'll not survive tons of bricks falling on top of you."

He took his time considering what I had just said. "Very well, Catherina. I will make him a bit more comfortable."

"Thanks." I heard the cell door open and some shuffling, after which the cell door banged close. "Tudor, how do you feel?"

"Better, much better."

"Thanks, Anubis," I said.

The jackal-headed vampire grunted.

"Anubis, how was Queen Eleonore able to change you and Ra?"

"I do not know. She took us to a cave and when I woke up, I had become what I am now. She did the same thing to Ra."

"A cave? Where?"

"I do not know."

"Where is Ra now?"

"In the palace somewhere." He waved his arm in an upward direction.

"Queen Eleonore must have a big court here at the palace, doesn't she?"

"Yes, she has."

"Besides you, Ra, Isolde, and Ladeena, who else is here?"

"Many more."

He didn't want to divulge any more information. I would have to try another angle.

"Anubis, where is Queen Eleonore now?"

"Out."

"When will she return?"

"Soon."

"Come on, you can say more than one word at the time."

He gave a small, wailing squeal.

"Are you in pain?" I asked.

"At times, yes. It is difficult to speak."

"I'm sorry, I didn't realize that."

"It's my lot in life."

"Is Tristan with the queen?" He was the vampire Isolde had mentioned earlier.

"Yes. I heard they went to a concert. In a cave."

"The same cave you mentioned before?"

"I don't know. Ra and I are just slaves here."

"And who else is with her right now?"

"Bogdan and Lucian."

Slowly, the information was trickling out.

"Any other ladies-in-waiting, besides Isolde and Ladeena?"

"Giselle and Klara."

That would make 13 vampires at her court. It didn't look good. There were too many of them, and maybe there were others. Anubis did not mention Nicolae and Ilie, so I was curious to see his reaction.

"Anubis, what role did—I mean—what role do Nicolae and Ilie play at Queen Eleonore's court?" I almost gave away that they were both dead.

He did not respond right away; instead, he walked to my cell, eyes curious and ears twitching. "You know about them?"

"I know about most of you," I said, unflinchingly looking into his dark eyes.

"They were the enforcers."

"You mean they punish, torture, and kill?"

Anubis nodded.

"Are you afraid of them?" I asked.

He nodded again.

"Is Ra afraid of them?"

"Everyone is afraid of them," he answered. "I heard they've gone missing. Vlady, too."

Of course they were missing, as in dead as door nails, covered with uranium powder and disintegrating in the deep pit Mundibuto had thrown them in.

"Do you feel better since they've gone missing?"

"Yes."

"Would you like to get away from here?"

"Even if I do, there is nowhere to go and hide."

"Is Ra of the same mind as you?"

"Yes, Ra and I are the lowest at the court."

"Any other vampires that you forgot to tell me about?"

"Trudy is her valet, and Ruxandra is her maid. And Dragomir, Sandor, and Mateo. That's all."

That brought the total to 18 vampires of different statuses and capabilities. "Who were the vampires who took us hostage in the parking lot outside the castle?"

"Dragomir, Sandor, Mateo, and maybe Trudy."

Wait. That was good news. I'd counted some of them twice. She had only 14 vampires.

"Thank you, Anubis. Besides Ilie and Nicolae, who else is a mean vampire?"

"Lucian, Ladeena, Dragomir, and Klara. Watch out for Lucian—he's the worst of all."

"Thank you. I'll keep that in mind." It was time to win this poor vampire over to my side. "I'm so sorry that you're in this predicament, Anubis."

"It's my lot in life."

"If I were queen around here, I would restore you to the way you used to be."

"Really?" He grabbed the bars, full of hope.

"Yes, and Ra, too."

"Ra would like that. But you are not the queen. You are not a vampire, just a mortal."

"I am of royal blood. Vlad the Impaler was my great-great-granduncle."

"That is true." He looked at me with reverence and bowed. "Your highness, do understand, I have to obey orders and do as I am told."

Calling me *your highness* was a good beginning, and although I had no intention of becoming a queen, I needed to bluff all the way until I could get this situation under control.

"I understand, Anubis. All I want you to do is not to hurt Dr. Lupu. Do you think you can do that for me?"

After some hesitation, he said, "Yes."

"Now, listen carefully. Things will change around here. You must not fear Vlady, Ilie, and Nicolae. They will not come to the queen's help. Can you keep a secret?"

"On my honor, your highness." He bowed.

"First, don't address me as your highness for right now. Just Cat."

He bowed again. I hoped he got it. I would be in deep trouble if the other vampires heard him addressing me as your highness.

"Good. Now listen—I sent Nicolae and Ilie on a mission. I'm not sure if they'll return in time to help me."

"What?" He took a step back. He couldn't believe that the two vampires were turncoats.

"Did you know that Nicolae and Ilie helped kill Vlad the Impaler 500 years ago?" Maybe a farfetched explanation would convince him. "Vlad the Fifth had placed a death sentence on them, and I was in possession of the curse that would have killed them. I showed them leniency when they swore their loyalty to me, and I sent them on a mission."

"Lucian will kill them," he said, terrified.

"I thought so, but they took Vlady as hostage. Lucian won't touch them."

"Brilliant." Something resembling a smile came over Anubis's snout.

That was a good, convincing explanation, and very true, except that Ilie, Nicolae, and Vlady's mission was in hell.

"All I want you to do is promise that you'll be on my side when the time comes to choose allegiances."

"I promise," he said without hesitation, and he pounded his fist over his heart.

"Good. Who else is fed up with Eleonore?"

"Uh, Mateo and Isolde, and Sandor. And Ra. Definitely Ra."

"Do you think Ra will take my side?"

"Maybe. I don't know."

"Here is what I want you to do. Go find some water and give it to Dr. Lupu to drink, and call Ra to visit me. I want to speak to him."

"Right away, your hi—Catherina."

Accompanied by Anubis, a muscular vampire with the head of a falcon approached my cell. Like Anubis, he wore just a loincloth around his waist and leather sandals.

"Hello, Ra," I greeted him, hoping that I would be able to convert him to my cause, just as I had convinced Anubis.

"Catherina," he bowed slightly, fixing me with his falcon eyes.

"Good—you know who I am."

"Anubis told me that you are the great-great-grandniece of Vlad the Impaler." He spoke with more ease than Anubis.

"That means I am of royal blood. I am here to claim my rightful place and become the queen of vampires." I astounded myself by claiming such a lofty goal, but lies and manipulation were all I had right now in my bag of tricks.

"And yet you are in the dungeon, behind bars. And you are a human, too."

I crossed my arms. "I am here because I wish to be here for the time being. I can get out anytime I wish."

"That I'll have to see," he gave a short, high-pitched snicker.

"Stand back," I ordered him. He and Anubis did as told. It was time to use my Strigoi to impress and command obedience.

I put my arms together horizontally, with my hands back to back, and in one smooth movement I parted them. The bars on my cell door bent sideways, creating a wide gap, as if an invisible jaws-of-life had opened them. I stepped outside the cell, feeling free.

Ra looked back and forth from the gap in the bars to me.

"Ra, listen," whispered Anubis. "Nicolae and Ilie are Catherina's servants, and they have Vlady."

Ra was shocked at what he heard. He stared disbelievingly at Anubis, who nodded to reinforce what he had just said. It must have been the right information because Ra and Anubis fell to their knees in front of me.

"What would you like us to do, your highness?" Ra asked in a fearful and respectful voice.

"I want you to secretly divulge my royal bloodline to the other vampires who are fed up with the queen. Tell them that I came here to mete out justice."

"Yes, we will do that." Ra glanced at Anubis to make sure he was in this as well. Anubis nodded.

"Good. And when the time comes, I expect both of you and other sympathetic vampires to be on my side."

"I promise," said Anubis.

"I promise," said Ra. "But may I remind you that you are not a vampire."

"If I wish to become a vampire, I can become a vampire."

Chapter 21. The Vampires

Angelique kicked the stone ball, but it wouldn't budge. It was jammed at the entrance. A circle could fit through a triangle, if its diameter were smaller. The damn ball was a hair larger. As angry as a vampire can get, she pulled her gun from her ankle holster and shot the rock at the points of interference. And then she kicked the ball again.

It started moving slowly, rolling toward the center of the triangular passage, and suddenly, the stone floor opened up and the ball dropped in.

But not completely. It was only halfway in, stuck in the opening and keeping the floor from closing back up.

"Guys, can you hear me?" she shouted from the triangular mouth of the passage.

"Loud and clear!" came François's acknowledgement from down below.

"What took you so long?" Mundibuto asked.

Assured that the trap was neutralized, she approached cautiously and peeked down through the gap. "I had to find the right-size ball."

"It looks good from down here," replied Mundibuto.

"Can you jump out?" she asked.

Before she had even finished her question, François came out halfway through a corner opening and then climbed out. Mundibuto threw the bags up to François and came up. Angelique squeezed over the ball and joined her friends on the other side. After quick embraces, happy to have overcome this latest trap, they exited from the triangular passage onto a ledge overlooking a colossal cave.

The cavern was dripping with stalactites, and the floor was forested with as many stalagmites. Some even connected in giant columns, giving the cave the appearance of a Gothic cathedral. The deadly quiet was disturbed by the sound of an occasional drip here and there. On the bottom, instead of a lake, there was a black hole surrounded by several stone boxes. Strange statues, resembling gargoyles, were posted on top of the stone boxes, as if keeping guard over them.

"This is a caver's dream," said François, turning his headlamp on.

"Or a caver's nightmare," added Angelique.

Mundibuto turned his headlamp on to shed some light in the vast chamber below them, but it barely made a difference in the huge cave.

"Do you think there are any more traps along the descending path?" Angelique used her flashlight to trace the trail to the bottom.

"We should not let our guards down," said Mundibuto, pulling a powerful flashlight from his bag. "Although I think we've reached our destination." He shone his light into the recesses of the cave, where burlap sacks hung by ropes off the lower ceilings like bats.

"What on Earth are those?" whispered Angelique, lighting the sacks with her flashlight.

"From what Cat's told me, those must be the zombies," answered Mundibuto.

"Why are they hung from the ceiling?"

Mundibuto shrugged. "Cat said that they are kept inside burlap sacks, hung upside down by their ankles."

François pulled his flashlight out of his bag. With their powerful beams of light, he and Mundibuto inspected the rest of the cave and alcoves, which were loaded with hanging sacks of zombies, numbering in the thousands.

François pointed his flashlight toward the bottom of the cave. "Those boxes circling the hole in the center—those seem to be stone sarcophagi. Twelve of them."

The black hole seemed to be a well of some kind, as far as they could tell. Two heavy chains came out of the well and connected around a sheave attached to the cave's ceiling.

"Should we take the path down?" Mundibuto shined his light's beam on the descending trail. "Someone cut out steps for easy walking. How thoughtful."

"After so many traps, I'm not sure what is safe here," said François, frowning.

"That stalactite-stalagmite column looks strong enough." Angelique stepped back and leaped 30 feet or more to cling onto the calcite column.

"Be careful, Angelique!" shouted François.

She descended along the rippled column with an agility of an ape and stood at its base, patting it to indicate its sturdiness. François and Mundibuto threw the bags down to her and they came down along the column, joining her.

Among the stalagmites, the gently sloping ground was littered with human bones—skulls, mandibles, ribs, femurs, shoulder blades, pelvic girdles, and vertebrae— whole or in pieces, and finger and feet joints piled like pebbles.

"Where do you think these came from?" François wondered.

Whatever they were seeing was not on ossuary or a massive grave. The bones, or perhaps originally the corpses, seemed to have been discarded like rubbish all around.

After another assessment of any signs of danger, they descended among the stalagmite formations to the flat, stony ground on which the twelve stone sarcophagi encircled the well in the center. Curiously, the floor was made of marble, inset with intricate designs of different colors, giving the impression of a religious sanctuary. They stepped cautiously onto the smooth floor and approached the stone sarcophagi.

With a thundering bang and dust bursting from several locations, including the triangle doorway from where they had come, large slabs of granite slammed down, entombing them.

Chapter 22. The Vampires

"We're trapped in here," said Angelique, looking up at where they'd come from.

"Not again," François said, as if bored with the same thing happening all over.

"What else should we have expected?" Mundibuto snickered and shook his head in disgust.

"This woman is diabolical. What is she trying to shelter in here, besides the zombies?" said François, and that was a lot, coming from a vampire who'd seen his share of evil doings. "This may be the entrapment of last resort—entombed with the stored goods." He opened his arms to indicate the stone boxes with the terrifying creatures on top of them, and the sacks with zombies hanging from the lower ceilings of adjacent niches.

Angelique didn't pay any attention to them. Instead, she stepped carefully, inspecting the floor. "Any of these patterns could have been the trigger to entomb us."

"Only a distorted mind could have built this!" raged François.

"You got that right. Look at these things." Mundibuto motioned toward a frightful creature, crouched down, with bat wings partly deployed, standing on top of the stone box in front of him.

"It is a statue of Satan, with its wings open and ready to take flight," scoffed François, walking around another blackened statue of a tall hominid with legs and hooves resembling those of a goat, claws instead of fingers, and a partially open, wolf-like mouth exposing long canine teeth.

On the statue's backside, he observed the scaly tail of a rat. He touched the tail. "There are sharp barbs at the end of each scale on this tail."

"Look at this—like a monk." Mundibuto pointed his flashlight at one statue standing at a height of seven feet or more, with its wings wrapped around it like a cloak, and resembling some Inquisition priest.

The others were in different positions: crouching, standing, or about to leap into the air.

"Twelve," said François, walking around. "One guardian on each sarcophagus. Anyone have any idea why they're here?"

"They're just statues," said Mundibuto.

François walked near a statue that was halfway crouched with its wings unfurled. "I don't think these are just statues. Check out the details. And the wings are like leather. My light almost shines through them."

"You're right," said Angelique. "I can see the veins in the wings." She climbed up to the statue and touched the surface of the wings. "They're not made of stone. The surface is not cold, like the stalactites. It feels as if they're made of plastic. I sense some kind of fine fuzz on the surface of the wings."

"Maybe they're made of fiberglass," proposed Mundibuto.

"This one is different," said François. "Instead of hooves, it has lion paws with unsheathed claws."

"If they're made of fiberglass, they are modern," said Angelique. "They could have been made in the past 50 years, I guess." She produced from one of her pockets a butane cigarette lighter and ignited it, exposing the flame to one of the spiky bones just underneath the leathery wing. Nothing burned, nothing melted. She moved the flame under the wing, and although she could see the light of the flame through the wing's skin, the material did not melt or crack. "It doesn't burn or melt," she said, jumping down from the box.

"So it's not fiberglass," said François, crossing his arms, puzzled by the statues. "And if these were mummified creatures, they would burn."

"Do you think these things were once alive?" Mundibuto's eyes widened.

Angelique shuddered. "These would be scarier than us vampires if they were in motion."

"Maybe, but they're dead now," said François. "Or they're just statues."

Mundibuto walked to the edge of the well, staring down into the immense darkness. "This hole in the ground may be the only way out." He pulled a road flare out of his pack, pulled the cap, ignited it, and tossed it down into the well.

François and Angelique joined him to observe the burning flare disappear into the dark void. Eventually the light died out, but without hitting the bottom of the well or its walls.

"That's one deep hole." Mundibuto sniffed the air. "There is a small draft coming from down below."

François looked at the doubled, heavy iron chains descending into the hole. "This could be attached to an elevator of some kind down there."

Their eyes followed the chains up all the way to the sheave on the ceiling. It seemed strong enough to support a heavy elevator box of some kind.

"I'll get down and see what's in the well," said Mundibuto, preparing to jump.

"I don't know," said François, rubbing the back of his neck. "Something is not right here."

Mundibuto looked at him inquisitively.

"Why entrap us, when there is this hole with a heavy iron chain going down into it?" François questioned. "It is as if someone were inviting us to take the only way out, for some reason."

Angelique shrieked. "Guys, one of the statues moved!"

"Moved? Which one? They seem to be standing where they were befo—" François didn't finish his sentence.

He, Angelique, and Mundibuto stared at the brown-black statues on the nearest stone boxes. Most seemed to be in the same position, although some had their heads and their bodies turned toward the vampires. The statues' liquid, black eyes focused on them.

Chapter 23. Cat

Isolde came to see me. I stood in my prisoner stance, holding onto the bars. I had straightened the bars back into their original position after Ra left. She stopped in front of my cell, her head slightly bowed.

"Catherina, the queen extends her apologies and has instructed me to escort you out of the dungeon to proper quarters."

I looked to see if she was alone, and she was by herself, without Ladeena. She had even sent Anubis out of the cell row, although it made no difference since the heavy wooden door was nothing but sawdust on the floor.

"Where is the tall broad, Ladeena?" I had to make sure she wasn't lurking somewhere in a dark corner.

"She was summoned by her majesty to join her."

"Hmm. So you came here to spring me out of jail."

"If you promise to behave, I'll take you to the upper chambers. I'll draw you a bath, give you fresh clothes, and provide whatever libation and nourishment you desire."

"With one condition." I raised a finger. "Release Tudor as well." I pointed sideways toward his cell.

She squirmed, looking back and forth from Tudor to me.

"Let me inspire you. You bring Dr. Tudor to the upper chambers. Have Anubis, or whatever his name is, stay with him at all times." I played dumb about Anubis's name on purpose. "Provide Dr. Tudor with food, drink, and a clean bed. And I promise I'll behave." I stared, waiting for her to respond.

"Only if he is in another chamber, away from you."

"Fair enough."

She turned to Anubis and ordered, "Open her cell."

"No need to bother." I bent open the bars, just as I had for Ra, and came out through the opening.

Isolde backed up against the opposite wall. I knew she had no trouble bending the bars herself, but without touching them, as I did—she must have thought it was pure dark magic.

I stopped in front of Tudor's cell. He was standing on the stool with the noose around his neck. He looked at me with sad eyes.

"Anubis!" I called the vampire, and he came into the cell row. "Take the ropes off Tudor's neck and wrists."

Anubis opened the cell door and did as he was told, while Isolde fretted nearby. Tudor came out and I gave him a big hug. Poor guy—the things he had to endure to be with me!

I whispered in his ear, "It will be OK. Trust me." I turned and looked at Isolde. "Lead the way."

She blinked nervously. For sure, she was not high on the totem poll at this court, and now I was giving her orders as well.

As she passed by to lead the way, I told Anubis, "Don't harm Tudor."

Anubis bowed. "Yes, Catherina."

Isolde turned her head in surprise at Anubis's response. That was good. She was becoming confused about who was in charge around here. With her skirts lifted, she escorted me up the stairs to the second floor to another chamber near the one with the ruined door. Anubis took Tudor to a chamber on the first floor.

My new chamber was opulent and had a private bathroom with indoor plumbing. Compliments of the 20th century, no doubt.

"Shall I draw you a bath, Catherina?"

"Go ahead, Isolde." A bath would be good to relax me. She opened the gold-plated faucets and filled the lion-clawed cast iron bathtub with water, after which she helped me out of my costume of a dress. I was even wearing a girdle, for crying out loud!

The water was warm as I stepped into the tub. I sank in, feeling the calming effect of the lavender-scented water.

"Shall I wash your hair, Catherina?"

Wash my hair? Yes, my hair needed washing, and I could wash my own hair. But I needed to establish a servant-master relationship here. Isolde was from the olden times, and she believed it was her duty to serve her master, or in this case, me, her mistress. I nodded and let her shampoo my hair.

"Isolde, are you related to Tristan?"

"He's my brother."

"How did you two become vampires?"

"Tristan was the queen's secretary. She convinced him to become like her, but he didn't want to be immortal without me."

"Did you want to become a vampire?"

"Living forever has its appeal, I must say." She rinsed my hair and then applied the conditioner.

"Do you bathe the queen as well?"

"No, not often. Ruxandra and Klara usually bathe her. Giselle helps her dress."

"But not Ladeena?"

"No, Ladeena is not—"

"Ladeena is not what?"

"Feminine enough."

She rinsed my hair again and began lathering me with a large sponge. Although a vampire, Isolde had tender fingers and gentle hands, but they were cold at first, until the water warmed them up.

"Are all the ladies-in-waiting with the queen right now?"

"Yes."

"Are all the gentlemen with her as well?"

She stopped sponging my toes and looked at me. "What gentlemen are you aware of?"

"Let's see. Lucian, Trudy, Bogdan, Dragomir, Mateo, Sandor, and Tristan."

"You know them all," she said in surprise. "Yes, they are with her, except for Mateo. He's around in the castle."

"Anubis and Ra don't go out frequently."

"Never. They are not allowed."

"Where did all of them go?"

She continued lathering me with the sponge and then she rinsed me. She wrapped my hair in a towel and then dried my body with a large fluffy white towel. Afterward, she dressed me in a white robe with a golden insignia. I had to admit, this pampering felt good. I indicated that I expected an answer to my question.

"I don't know for sure where they went. Somewhere in the Carpathian Mountains."

Well, this part was good, but I had to take control over the next details before I got dressed.

"Isolde, please bring me a bottle of mineral water," I said, dismissing her.

After I finished the final details of my beauty routine, I returned to the bedroom and on the bed I found a flouncy pink silk dress and all the paraphernalia of the old-fashioned undergarments.

Isolde came in with a bottle of mineral water and a crystal glass on a silver tray. "May I pour you some water, Catherina?"

"Please." I observed how elegantly she poured the water. She had definitely been trained for the court.

"May I help you to dress?"

I couldn't possibly get into that dress all by myself. The corset, which I didn't need, had laces on the back that needed to be tightened by someone else. But I didn't want to get dressed in those period clothes again. "Why are you giving me this dress?"

"Would you like to wear something else in the palace?"

"My own clothes."

"That short skirt?" Her expression showed she disapproved of my miniskirt.

"In the car I arrived in with Tudor, I have my luggage. Bring it to me, please."

"Right away, Catherina." She left to retrieve my bags.

I sat on the edge of the bed with my arms folded. I began to worry. Why was she so much nicer now? Obviously, the queen had told her to treat me like a distinguished guest, which I intended to play to the hilt. Or she felt inferior to me and therefore more obedient. Or it was all a ruse.

Chapter 24. Cat

After Isolde brought me my bag with my clothes, I dressed in my black jeans, black T-shirt, and black sneakers. I was ready for action. Isolde placed the pink dress into the wardrobe and stood by the door, as if waiting to be dismissed. We had to have a talk.

"Have a seat, Isolde."

She looked unsure. I helped her by pointing to the tall-backed chair between the fireplace and the window. I sat on the opposite chair, closer to the door, intentionally trying to make her feel trapped.

"What's happened since last time we saw each other?" I phrased an open question so I could observe her guessing what answer I wanted to hear.

"What do you—I don't know—"

"Tell me what happened after you and Ladeena left me in the dungeon."

"We talked to the queen, and when she heard that Ladeena had put you in a cell, she was furious. She told me to take care of you like a proper lady. Then she ordered Ladeena and the others to join her immediately."

"Do you know who I am?"

"You are Catherina. The queen ordered Mateo, Dragomir, Sandor, and Trudy to bring you and Dr. Lupu to the castle and to hold you until she returned. That's all I know."

"Isolde, for your information, I am Catherina Draculesti Sanders, the great-great-granddaughter of Vlad V Draculesti. Did you know him?"

"Yes, I knew him. But I didn't know that you and he were related. Is it true that he died?"

"That is true. And I am the great-great-grandniece of Vlad the Impaler. Do you know what that means?"

Her eyes widened and, to my surprise, she kneeled in front of me. "Forgive me, your excellence. I didn't know of your royal blood." She stared at the floor.

Now we were on the right track. I was royalty, which she took very seriously, and she was my subject. I was going to make her take my side.

"I forgive you. Please sit down."

She did as instructed, looking meekly at me.

"Tell me everything you know about this court, and start with Vlady, Ilie, and Nicolae."

She was taken aback when I mentioned their names. "Uhh…Vlady is the queen's lover. Nicolae and Ilie are in the queen's guard. We haven't heard from them for a week, and I think the queen is looking for them."

"Has that happened before?"

"Not for this long."

"What gossip do you know about these three?"

"Gossip? Like what?"

"Come on, Isolde—court politics, rumors, that kind of information."

"The queen wasn't happy with Vlady. She suspected that he was fooling around with human women, and she had begun fancying Dragomir lately."

"Was Vlady upset about that?"

"He didn't seem to be bothered by such rumors. He's even made advances to me."

"What about Nicolae and Ilie?"

"They like human women."

"No, other than that."

The corners of her mouth turned down while her eyebrows went up. "They, along with Lucian, Dragomir, and Bogdan, are in the queen's guard."

"Taking care of her army?"

"Do you know about that army?"

"Yes, tell me what *you* know about that army."

"It is an unholy army of the dead, zombies. That's what I heard." She looked frightened.

"Just zombies?"

She nodded. "Yes. They are held in some cave in the mountains."

That was news to me. They were held in a cave, not in a crypt under a cemetery. Could it be that the queen wasn't aware of the army under the cemetery in Sighisoara? Could Vlady, Ilie, and Nicolae have been engaged in treasonous undertakings? That was something to keep in mind.

"Where are the proto-vampires held?"

"Proto-what?" She looked honestly perplexed.

My suspicion of Vlady, Nicolae, and Ilie increased. They were involved in building an army without the queen's knowledge. "You've never heard of proto-vampires?"

She shook her head in earnest. "The only other thing I heard, and that was a rumor, was that in the cave where the zombies are held live twelve guardians."

It was my time to be surprised. "Guardians?

"They're supposed to be worse than zombies."

"Who are they guarding?" I asked.

"The eternal resting places of the dark gods."

Chapter 25. The Vampires

"Their eyes. They're alive," said Angelique.

The eyes of the statues were wet and shiny like glass. They were completely black—onyx black, without any white showing—like those of predatory animals.

"They seem to be focused on us," Mundibuto said from the edge of the well. "Angelique, why don't you walk to the other side of the sarcophagi, and let's see what happens."

Angelique did not pass between two of the stone boxes; instead, she jumped more than 20 feet up into the air and landed on the other side. She came down facing the nearest sarcophagus, and the crouched statue on that box pinned her with its eyes. She looked to the right, and that statue was glaring at her, and so was the one to the left.

"Have you observed these three?" She motioned to the statues in front of her.

"Yes, I see them with their heads turned toward you, but I didn't see the heads moving," said François, motioning to Mundibuto to spread out.

Mundibuto walked around the well to the opposite side and looked at the statues closest to him. They were all looking at him. "Did you see them moving, François?"

"No. They were so fast—one moment they were looking at me, and the next at you. Fascinating creatures, whatever they are. Let's do one last test." François jumped up to the lowest stalactite above them and clung to it. He looked down, only to see four pairs of black liquid eyes staring up at him.

"Instant motion?" Mundibuto said from down below.

"Instant repositioning," said Angelique. "Or perhaps metamorphosing?"

François eyed the three bags left on the other side of the boxes. This situation required axes, and Mundibuto had placed one in every bag. "I think we'd better grab the axes." He hurled himself near the bags and quickly pulled the axes out, throwing one to Angelique and the other to Mundibuto.

Angelique caught her double-blade axe, but the statue on the box in front of Mundibuto caught his axe. The statue never took its eyes off Mundibuto.

"Hey! That's my axe!" Mundibuto jumped onto the sarcophagus, nose to nose with the statue.

But before he could even blink, Mundibuto found himself locked against the statue's body. The axe's handle was behind his back, and the two skeletal arms holding onto the handle pinned him in a stranglehold. The statue looked him straight in the eyes. Mundibuto pushed against its chest, but its grip tightened. Understanding the futility of fighting such a creature, Mundibuto pushed back harder and broke the wooden axe handle, freeing himself. He jumped down onto the ground, away from whatever those creatures were. "That was bad," he said, walking around to dissipate his shock.

"Let's see if they bleed." François jumped up and, with all his strength, brought his axe down to cleave one statue from head to crotch.

His axe didn't reach its destination. The statue caught the axe's blade with one hand, while with the other he grabbed

François by the ankle. The steel blade was implanted in the statue's hand, and François hung by his ankle, unsure of what to do next. He wriggled to get lose, but the statue squeezed its grip.

"Angelique, cut off his arm!" he shouted.

Angelique jumped up over the other statues, and as she came down, she threw the axe against the arm holding François. The statue let go of François and caught the other axe. Both she and François landed on the ground and quickly distanced themselves from the satanic statues holding their axes by the blades.

"Thanks, Angelique, and good move throwing the axe at his arm. Otherwise, it would have caught you, too," said François.

"I figured that while in the air. But let's see if they can stop bullets." She pulled her gun from her ankle holster and fired—click, click. "Damn it." She remembered that she had fired the bullets against the stone ball, and now her gun was empty.

Mundibuto jumped over and landed near François, with his gun drawn. "At this one's head!" he shouted, and he and François fired several rounds together. But the statue moved its head and the bullets missed. "Anywhere!" he shouted. They showered the statue with all the bullets in their guns, and some went through the statue's body but left no trace of bullet holes.

"Did you hit the darn thing?" Angelique asked.

"Yes, we did, but holes opened instantly in its body, ahead of the oncoming bullets, and let them through," said Mundibuto.

"*Mon dieu*. These things are devils," said François. "We won't be able to destroy them."

"Question is, what are they?" Angelique wondered.

"They are quicker and stronger than vampires," agreed Mundibuto.

"Yes, steel won't cut them, and lead goes through them like it's going through air," said François. "Let's hope they stay where they are right now."

"We won't have a chance if they get down and come after us," said Mundibuto.

"I don't think they will come down off the sarcophagi," Angelique said.

"Why not?" Mundibuto asked.

"I think they're guarding the sarcophagi and whatever they contain," she said.

Mundibuto, François, and Angelique stood together, staring at the statue creatures. And the statues were all standing now, with their wings half open, staring back at them.

"Those things are definitely some kind of guardians," said François.

Chapter 26. The Vampires

"Who do you think is buried in there?" Mundibuto approached his friends, worried about the occupants in the stone boxes.

"You and Angelique became vampires after you were contaminated from the sarcophagus unearthed in Egypt," said François. "Vlad V, whose vampire strain I carry, was contaminated from another tomb that was here in Transylvania. That tomb contained a devil-like corpse and was located under Vlad V and his uncle's cell, where King Corvinus had imprisoned them. What if these sarcophagi contain similar creatures?"

"Is that who's inside the sarcophagi?" Mundibuto wondered.

"It is not who, but what, that is inside these boxes," replied François.

"Jesus," muttered Mundibuto.

"It is time to become religious," said Angelique.

"And those things also control the statues," Mundibuto speculated. "Something similar to Strigoi, which Cat controls."

"Possibly," agreed François. "Except these Strigoi are encased in statues."

"Why is that?" wondered Angelique. "Why not have undefined shapes, like Cat's Strigoi?"

"These statues will scare people away," Mundibuto said. "And what else would you have on your coffin to protect you but the shape of the devil himself?"

"The statues might be replicas of the inhabitants inside the boxes," François ventured to guess.

"We're fucked," said Angelique. "We are trapped in here and have no way of fighting these things."

"They haven't attacked us yet," said François. "Their task is to protect their masters."

"Maybe we should get the hell out of here," said Angelique. "Force our way out somehow."

"If Eleonore finds out—and I'm sure she will find out—that we discovered this cave, it will be war," said François.

"Angelique's right, let's get the hell out of here," Mundibuto said. "We have a better chance of fighting her outside this cave."

"And the zombies?" François pointed to the hanging sacks.

"We live to destroy them another day."

"Why not destroy them now, while they're hibernating?" said François. "There are thousands of them. If they wake up anytime soon, their sheer numbers will overwhelm us."

"How do you suggest we get rid of them?" Angelique asked.

"Did Cat tell you how she killed them?" François asked Mundibuto.

"It was a luminescent fog caused by Vlad's ashes. That fog burned all of them to coarse grains of ash, like sand."

"Let's set a few on fire and see what happens. They seem dry enough to burn," said Angelique. She flipped her lighter on and observed the flame. "There is a draft of fresh air in this cave. There should be enough oxygen to keep them burning."

"Wait," said François. "I want to see what they look like." He ran to the nearest and lowest hanging sack, jumped up, and cut the rope.

The sack fell to the floor, making a sound like pieces of wood dropped onto a hard surface. François slashed the sack opened and shook its contents out. Mundibuto and Angelique joined him to see the zombie. It was a female with blonde hair, and it looked as shriveled as a mummy. The skin was dark brown, like well-worn leather. Her body was covered in rags of rough yarn similar to the sack she was held in.

"Oh, God," said Angelique, revolted. "I'm going to go to church more often."

François squatted down near the zombie and moved her chin with the blade of his knife.

She opened her eyes. They were red as rubies.

Before he had time to react, she grabbed François by the wrist and pulled herself to his throat to bite him. François jumped up, pulling along the skeletal creature. He swung the zombie over his head and slammed her onto the ground like a rug. One of her legs shattered, but she didn't lose her grip on François. With a quick chop of his hand he broke her arm, but the hand stayed clutched onto his wrist.

The zombie got up on one knee, stood on the broken leg, and hobbled toward François, reaching with her other good arm. Her jaw was moving as if trying to say something. From behind, Mundibuto kicked the back of her neck. Her head broke loose and tumbled down. The jaw kept moving on the head, as if it were spring-loaded. The headless body kept approaching François. Angelique flipped her lighter and set her rags on fire. The zombie ignited like a torch and collapsed in a bundle of flames. Mundibuto stomped on the head, cracking the skull and putting an end to the macabre moving jaw.

Without saying a word, the three of them began setting the sacks on fire. The flames engulfed the sacks, and screeches came from inside as the fire began consuming them. Many of the sacks broke, disgorging the burning zombies, which fell on the ground. Many tried to push themselves up, but the flames overcame them and they collapsed, burning like piles of rags.

"Thank God they're flammable!" shouted Angelique.

Mundibuto, Angelique, and François fanned out and continued igniting the sacks. The vampires had to jump up to reach that ones that were too high. They hung onto each one to ignite them and then swung to the next zombie sack. The cave became an inferno of burning sacks and zombie bodies. Some burned on the ropes, while many others fell to the ground in flames. A few managed to walk aimlessly while ablaze. The deafening shrieks of terror coming from the intact sacks echoed in the cave.

"We need to set them on fire faster," shouted Mundibuto. "They're awakening. Check in the bags—there are butane torches in there."

Each one of them ran to the bags and found the torches.

"Spread out!" shouted François. "Set a ring of fire from inside outward."

The plan was to start the zombies in the inner circle on fire and, in case the ones beyond would awaken, they would catch fire as well. They moved as quickly as vampires could move, and with the butane torches they set the sacks on fire much faster. But they were too many of them, and the awakening of the zombies began en masse.

Soon it was no longer necessary to jump to reach them. They dropped down like rotten fruit after ripping themselves out of their sacks and slashing with their teeth the ropes that held them suspended by their ankles. The zombies were no threat to the vampires, except for their numbers and the fact that even body parts were grasping, trying to restrain them.

The three vampires realized that kicking, punching, and tearing them apart was not going to stop the zombies from attacking them. Fire was still the ultimate solution. Each vampire caught a zombie or two by their feet, set them on fire, and spun the burning and screaming zombies into other zombies, setting them ablaze. It took them over an hour to set them all on fire.

The cave was an inferno, ablaze with fire and smoke and crawling limbs that escaped the torches. Once there weren't any more standing or screaming zombies, the three gathered the squirming limbs and threw them into a bonfire to eliminate any trace of them.

They sat down around the stinking fire, and occasionally one of them would spy another arm crawling around like a crab, which they would quickly throw into the flames.

"Hiking is not hiking without a bonfire," said François.

"I forgot to pack the marshmallows," said Mundibuto.

"Did we get rid of all of them?" Angelique looked over her shoulder.

"I think so," said François, checking the ceilings as well. "The good thing is that the smoke is dissipating fast."

Just as he said that a rumble started deep inside the mountain, and the chains over the well started moving.

Chapter 27. The Vampires

A few minutes later, a round black iron elevator cab rose from the well. It resembled a steam boiler, with many rivets dotting its surface. A round porthole was mounted on the large door recessed in the cab's body. The two chains went through its roof's center.

"The dragon is coming home," said Angelique.

"It was about time," said Mundibuto.

"Take cover," said François.

They hid behind the stone boxes, waiting.

After coming to a complete stop, the elevator's door opened inward and a mean-looking vampire—tall, broad-shouldered, dressed in black leather, with a shaved head and dark thick eyebrows—appeared, holding a machine gun in each hand. He stepped out and surveyed the cave, which was still illuminated by the last burning fires of the zombies.

"Lights!" he ordered.

From the top of the cab, large beams of light flooded the cave in all directions. After him, two more leather-clad vampires came out, each holding two machine guns as well. These two had dark and slick combed-back hair, and they looked as if they had never smiled in their lives.

"All clear back here," someone said from behind the elevator in a high-pitched voice. Another door had opened on the opposite side, and another crew, just like the first one, exited and surveyed the cave on that side.

"Three of them are on this side!" boomed the large vampire. "Show yourselves! You don't stand a chance against us!"

Other vampires poked the barrels of their guns from the left and right sides of the round cab. Another one, with his hair parted in the middle like a professor, was on the roof, holding two machine guns. They were armed for bear.

"I see them," said the one on top of the elevator in his high-pitched voice. "They're behind the burial boxes."

The vampires on either side of the elevator sprinted in the blink of an eye and took cover behind the other stone boxes and then farther behind the stalagmites. The statues on the stone boxes nearby fixed them with their eyes but did not take any action against them.

"We have them surrounded, your majesty," said the large vampire, addressing someone inside the elevator.

Ladeena came out first, dressed as for fox hunting in high boots, followed by Eleonore, dressed in a red jacket with gold trim, shiny boots, and golden spurs. Last to come out were two more vampire women, dressed in red jackets and boots as well.

Queen Eleonore, with her beehive white wig and a hunter's hat on top of it, walked calmly near two sarcophagi, the closest path to François, Mundibuto, and Angelique's hiding spots. "Now listen, you out there. I don't know yet who you are, although I have a good idea, but I suggest you come out with your hands up. Or Dragomir here and the rest of my royal guard will start shooting. And they won't stop until you are all dead."

Eleonore looked around the cave and finally saw the devastation caused by the fire. She turned whiter than her already vampire-pale complexion. "What the hell have you done?"

"Shit, no! They incinerated the zombies!" shouted a woman vampire, as the others looked aghast at the smoldering bodies. The vampires spoke to each other in soft agitated whispers.

François, Mundibuto, and Angelique exchanged worried glances. Six male vampires, one even larger than Mundibuto, holding rapid-fire machine guns surrounded them. A pissed-off vampire queen and four more vampire women were ready to kill them for what they'd done. The odds of overpowering them or even surviving this were not much better than the zombies' odds had been earlier.

"I'm going to count to three, and you'd better come out!" boomed the big vampire, Dragomir.

Silently, François, Mundibuto, and Angelique agreed among themselves to surrender. They stood up with their hands in the air.

"We're surrendering," said Angelique. "Don't get crazy."

Chapter 28. The Vampires

Mundibuto, Angelique, and François came toward the elevator from different directions, passing between the stone sarcophagi, stopping in front of Eleonore's vampires. As they approached, they could feel the eyes of the guardians fixed on them. They hoped that those damn things would not join the armed vampires.

"François, darling, gorgeous as usual." Eleonore smiled sourly. "You're blond now. Tsk, tsk. You disappoint me," she said in a condescending tone. "And you have with you the black rat, Mundibuto. How did you get out of the rat hole, rat?"

"That's what rats do, your queenliness," Mundibuto smirked.

"And I presume this is Angelique, the famous redhead Angelique. Except you've dyed your hair black now. I will so enjoy it when you're giving me foot massages."

Angelique closed the fingers of her right hand, leaving only the middle one to salute her.

"Watch it, you bitch!" hollered Dragomir, pointing his guns at her.

"Pathetic," said Eleonore, pushing his guns down. "Why did you come here, François?"

"For the love of caves. And what a cave this is!" François looked around in mocking admiration.

"You're after my kingdom, you usurper. Vlad died, and you think you're the new king, isn't that it?" Her face contorted in hatred. "But Vlad didn't have the right to anoint you, commoner." She spat in disgust. "Explain why you've burned my zombies!" She waved her arms in exasperation.

"Allow me to be polite," said François, spreading his arms as if ready to embrace her. "Nice to see you, Eleonore. You haven't changed at all over the eighty years since I last saw you. You don't look a day over 300. And who are all these courtiers looking as if they're on a fox hunt?"

"Fox hunt?" She chuckled. "We caught the foxes, for sure. Are these two your royal court?" She glanced spitefully at Angelique and Mundibuto.

"They are my friends," replied François.

"And now you are my prisoners," said Eleonore in a cold voice. "Why did you burn my zombies?"

"I didn't know they were your zombies. You should have placed a tag on them. Property of Queen Eleonore, or something. Besides, they looked like the living dead, freaks of nature."

"Well, they were my zombies, and it took me many years to make them."

"Why zombies?" François asked naively. "They don't stand a chance against vampires."

"Not vampires, you fool!" she shouted back. "A deterrent against people, humans."

"Eleonore, I'm at a loss. By the looks of it, you have a few good vampires to protect you, not to mention the proto-vampires."

"What proto-vampires? I don't see any proto-vampires around here."

"I say we should kill them here and now," said the vampire with the high-pitched voice from the top of the elevator cab.

The queen turned around and shouted, "Shut up, Lucian! I'll give you the chance to torture and kill them." She turned back to look at François. "What proto-vampires are you talking about?"

"Why ask me? They were yo—"

"Weren't you a proto-vampire before you became a vampire?" Lucian cut him off.

Eleonore looked at Lucian and then back at François. "Ahh, I see. Why not have armies of proto-vampires instead of zombies? Was that your question?"

François turned and looked at Mundibuto.

"Why are you looking at the black vampire?" she asked.

"Don't you have any proto-vampires?" Mundibuto asked.

"Why would I have proto-vampires? What a foolish idea." She held her forehead for a moment, thinking. "And that reminds me, Mundibuto, how did you get out of the hole Vlady, Ilie, and Nicolae shoved you in?"

"I'm a rat. You said so yourself."

"Where are Vlady, Ilie, and Nicolae?" she shouted at him.

"In a very safe place," said Mundibuto with a hint of smile.

"You were a decoy, weren't you? Angelique and François sprung you free and then the three of you captured my best and oldest vampires." Eleonore pointed a finger at them.

"That can't be!" Lucian jumped down, trembling with fury and ready to fire his guns.

"If you don't want them harmed, you'd better put your guns down," said Angelique.

"What? You've captured them? You vermin!" Lucian shouted.

"We can do a fair exchange—the three of us for the three of them," said François.

"Huh. You seem to forget that you are outnumbered and outgunned," replied Eleonore.

"And they are chained to a ton of dynamite. All Cat has to do is push a button," said Mundibuto.

Eleonore straightened up and cackled. "Catherina has them?" She laughed some more, and most of her vampires joined in.

"What's so funny?" Angelique asked.

"You may be vampires, but you are stupid vampires." Eleonore shook her head as if in disappointment. She pulled her cell phone from her belt. "You may find this recording disheartening, but you must hear it."

She tapped on the screen and raised it for them to hear what she had recorded earlier:

"What's the meaning of this, Eleonore?" It was Cat's voice.

"Now, now. That is not the proper manner in which to speak to a queen, is it?" Eleonore's voice responded.

"Why did you kidnap Dr. Lupu and me?"

"For your own protection, my dear."

Smiling, Eleonore turned off the phone, pleased with herself. "Well, then. I have Cat and the doctor in my custody. As for you three, I'll move you into more appropriate accommodations for further questioning. You'd better do as you're told." Eleonore snapped her fingers and, with her ladies-in-waiting, she returned to the elevator.

"Dragomir, bring out the boxes!" Lucian screeched.

The other five vampires closed in on their prisoners.

Mundibuto, François, and Angelique exchanged concerned glances. For the moment, they had their hands free, although they had no weapons. The boxes meant strong boxes, the only way to keep a vampire captive. This would be the last time that they would have any freedom of action, before they were to be enclosed in the boxes. They were three against five armed vampires. But one, the biggest of them, was in the elevator, bringing out the strong boxes.

The time to act was approaching.

Dragomir came out of the elevator, holding the first box. It was a gray, casket-size steel box, which he dropped onto the ground. He returned to the elevator to bring out the rest.

"Tristan, unlatch the lid," Lucian ordered.

An owlish-looking vampire gave his two guns to another vampire, bent down, and began spinning a wheel on the strong box's lid.

In an instant, Mundibuto, François, and Angelique sprang onto their assailants.

Chapter 29. The Vampires

It was not a fair fight. One vampire, Tristan, was bent down, unlocking the lid; another vampire held four machine guns in his arms, unable to fire any of them; the three other vampires had their guns pointing at their captives, but each was looking at Tristan turning the wheel on the box.

Mundibuto, François, and Angelique jumped on them with such speed and force that each opponent flew backward, letting go of some of their guns.

Mundibuto attacked Lucian and propelled him backward into the vampire who held the four guns. That vampire ended up on his back underneath Lucian, while Mundibuto jumped again and squatted on top of Lucian. Not wasting a millisecond, Mundibuto pulled one gun from Lucian's hand and, using the machinegun like a jackhammer, he discharged the entire magazine into Lucian's stomach and into the other vampire underneath him, who most likely took all the lead into his belly after it passed through Lucian. Bullets can go only so far through two vampire bodies.

Angelique rammed the vampire in front of her in the crotch, making him fly backward, landing between two sarcophagi farther away. She jumped up high to land on the fallen vampire, but one of the guardian statues extended an arm, blocking her, and she fell short of the mark. Nevertheless, she landed on her feet, but the other vampire was up, raising his machine gun to spray her with bullets.

She twisted and bent quicker than he was able to squeeze the trigger. She jumped out of the way, and none of the bullets hit her. She took cover behind a sarcophagus, planning her next move.

François flew at the last vampire holding two machine guns. He grabbed him by the neck, spun him and pounded him down over Tristan, who at that moment had just lifted the lid. The vampire still holding one machine gun fell into the open strongbox. François quickly grabbed Tristan's throat and launched him into the elevator's wall headfirst. The impact dented the wall. Then François pushed down on the lid with his foot with such force that one of the vampire's arms hanging out of the box broke, and he let his gun roll onto the ground. François kicked the limp arm into the box, jumped on the lid, and turned the locking wheel shut on that vampire. Having disposed of both vampires, he grabbed the fallen machine gun and, while running, he fired at Angelique's assailant. The bullets hit the vampire and he fell backward, rolled over, and ran for cover—hurt but not out of commission.

Dragomir came out of the elevator holding the second strong box, and when he saw the mayhem outside, he threw the box at Mundibuto, who caught it and swung it back at Dragomir, hitting him in the chest. Dragomir was the bigger and stronger vampire, and he didn't even take a step back from the heavy blow. Instead, he pushed it back at Mundibuto, who jumped over it at Dragomir. The blows and the kicks between the two of them came in rapid-fire succession. With just dust and pieces of clothing exploding outward neither one of them slowed down or retreated.

The commotion outside alerted the female vampires of the fight. They jumped to their feet when they heard the thump Tristan made as he smashed on the elevator wall, just before Dragomir moved the strong box out through the door.

"Giselle to the right. Klara and Ruxandra to the left. Ladeena with me on the roof." Eleonore barked the orders.

They grabbed Uzis and bolted out through the back exit as ordered. The queen and Ladeena jumped onto the roof, surveying the fight. Unfortunately for Giselle, she caught a boot heel to the throat from Angelique. Angelique twisted the gun from her hand and plunged it into Giselle's mouth, but before she could kill her, Angelique felt bullets raining down around her from above.

Angelique ran in the opposite direction, hugging the elevator's wall, and when she came to the other exit, she saw Tristan picking up an Uzi inside, getting ready to join the fight. She shot Tristan with all the bullets left in her gun. He fell to the floor, squirming. She pulled the gun from Tristan's hands and cautiously came out, searching for the shooter on the roof. She felt a blow to her head. Ladeena had just landed on top of her.

François stopped searching for the wounded vampire, saw Mundibuto and Dragomir pounding each other as if in a blur, and then spotted the queen and Ladeena on the roof. He raised his gun to fire, only to hear bullets buzzing by him from the other side of the elevator. He twisted and dropped flat on the ground, crawling for shelter. Near the elevator he saw the two women, Klara and Ruxandra, who had shot at him. He aimed carefully with the machine gun and sprayed them with bullets. They ran for cover among the stone sarcophagi and returned fire.

Angelique saw Ladeena bending down over her with the gun pointing at her head.

"Shoot her in the mouth like she wanted to shoot me!" screamed Giselle.

Ladeena took her eyes off Angelique for a moment to look at Giselle, and that's all Angelique needed. She jabbed her fingers into Ladeena's eyes, while at the same time she kicked her in the stomach, thrusting her several feet into the air. Ladeena shrieked with pain and covered her eyes, and as she came down, Angelique shot her in the chest. She rolled over so as not to be crushed by the blinded vampire. Giselle began firing at Angelique and she fired back, while both were running for cover.

Queen Eleonore stared, incredulous at what she was seeing down below. Dragomir and Mundibuto continued exchanging blows, neither one backing off an inch. They moved too fast for her to fire without hitting both of them. Angelique was hidden behind a sarcophagus, trading gunfire with Giselle. Ladeena was squirming on the ground, badly hurt. In another direction, her maid, Ruxandra, and her other lady-in-waiting, Klara, were exchanging fire with François. Aside from Dragomir, who was the only one standing but intensely engaged, her other male vampires were either dead or neutralized. One of the strong boxes was rocking wildly down below. She had underestimated Vlad's friends. There was no time to threaten them with harm against Cat. She had to appeal to the ultimate survival solution.

Eleonore raised her arms and howled at the top of her lungs for a minute or more. Some of the gunfire stopped, but not Mundibuto and Dragomir, who had no time to wonder where the howling was coming from.

The moment she stopped howling, all the statues on the sarcophagi began moving, crackling like twisted cellophane. Their forms turned into a dark fluid, like used motor oil. They looked at her, awaiting orders.

"Immobilize the traitors!" she commanded.

Instantly, the statues jumped off the sarcophagi and, in groups of four, approached François, Mundibuto, and Angelique.

The first group encircled Mundibuto and Dragomir. They clasped arms, making a ring that became smaller and smaller until the two were sandwiched in without any room to hit each other. Dragomir was squeezed out. Mundibuto felt fluid arms around his neck, arms, torso, legs, his entire body, completely immobilizing him as if he were in a liquid iron shroud.

The second group approached Angelique. She saw them and squeezed her last few rounds into one of them, but to no avail. Before she could react she was enveloped in a liquid iron wrap.

François ran out of bullets and, while the queen was howling like a beast from hell, he searched around for new weapons. He was crouching when he ran across one of the statue's feet. He had no time to jump away as the statue unmolded, embracing him tightly in its fluid body.

François, Mundibuto, and Angelique found themselves completely immobilized but aware of what was happening around them. The statues were holding them in a horizontal position at hip level, as if holding gurneys for further orders.

The queen jumped down and inspected the damage. Trudy, her valet, was liberated from the strongbox, one arm hanging limply. Lucian and Sandor lay on the ground out of commission, trying to heal from the wounds in their stomachs. Bogdan was peppered with bullets but faring better. And Tristan, her secretary, was in as bad shape as Lucian and Sandor.

Ladeena was blinded and shot. She was in a fetal position, covering her injured eyes. Ruxandra, her maid, and Giselle and Klara, her ladies-in-waiting, had a variety of bullet wounds, but none were serious.

Eleonore stomped her foot in distress. "Put the bastards in the strong boxes!" she ordered. "We'll deal with them later at the palace."

Dragomir brought out the third strongbox. François, Mundibuto, and Angelique were dropped, one in each box, and the lids were shut and locked. Each was imprisoned in a dark steel box.

Chapter 30. Cat

I did my best to win Isolde over to my cause, but she wasn't convinced that I had any chance against the queen. I couldn't fault her; I wasn't a vampire.

There were only four vampires on the premises, so I had a window of opportunity to escape from the castle. There was no other alternative. I might not get to see daylight again, but I had to strike before the queen came back.

Two vampires, Ra and Anubis, were on my side. Isolde was sitting on the fence. And I hadn't met Mateo yet. I had to lay my cards on the table and see how the four would react about my coup d'état or escape, whichever was easier. A coup d'état, with me as their proposed new queen, had a good one percent chance of succeeding. Escaping had a slightly better chance. When you're desperate and almost dead, you'll try anything. And I had one more ace in the hole.

"Isolde, would you bring over Mateo, Anubis, and Ra?"

After blinking a few times, Isolde asked, "Anubis and Ra, here?"

"Do you have another chamber where the five of us can meet?"

"Yes. No. I'll check."

"What's the matter?"

"Catherina, you may not know this, but Anubis and Ra are not allowed above the first floor."

"They're allowed in my castle," I said. "Is there a good meeting room on the second floor?"

"Yes, the day sitting room."

"Let's get to it."

I stood up and motioned with my head to do as I told her. Isolde took me to the day sitting room, which was a comfortable place with a large fireplace on the stone wall. The wood floor was covered with a plush carpet, and several dark-brown velvet sofas and chairs were positioned around a low oak coffee table. The other walls, which were whitewashed, were covered with tapestries of hunting scenes. Floor lamps, one in each corner, softly lit the room. The velvety red drapes on the windows on either side of the fireplace were closed.

I sat down near the fireplace in a comfortable wing chair, crossed my legs, and motioned to Isolde to get to it. What I was about to do was totally crazy, but it was better than giving up.

Isolde brought Mateo in first. He had his beret in his hand, and he was dressed in a wrinkled brown suit. He looked like a simple vampire who had never transitioned from the plain man he once was.

"Catherina, this is Mateo."

"Your excellence." Mateo bowed. "You have to understand that I followed orders when I captured you in the parking lot. I meant no harm."

"Nice to meet you, Mateo. You don't need to be worried. Had you ever met my great-great-grandfather Vlad the Fifth?"

"Yes, yes, I did. Sorry to see him gone." He twisted his beret in his hands.

"Have a seat." I pointed to the sofa on the opposite side of the coffee table. He sat quietly.

"Where are the others?" I raised an eyebrow at Isolde. She curtsied and left without a word. "Well, Mateo. How long have you been at Queen Eleonore's court?"

"I used to be her horses' caretaker, when the queen was a human, and afterward when we had horse-drawn carriages, your excellence."

"She made you into a vampire?"

He nodded. "Over the objections of Lord Vlad."

"Did you want to become a vampire?"

He shifted uncomfortably in his place. "At the time, well, no. I had a family, and I couldn't see them again. But now after centuries of it, it doesn't matter."

"Would you die for your queen?"

He sat up straight. "Your excellence, vampires don't die."

"They can be killed."

"I don't know. That question was never asked of me before."

"Do you like living forever?"

"Yes, I think so." He nodded.

157

"Good." I smiled at him.

The door opened, and Isolde brought Anubis and Ra inside. Mateo gave the two a long look, dismayed to see them in this room. Frankly, given the primitive, dirty, and monstrous looks of these two—one with a jackal's head and the other with a falcon's head—it was odd to see them in civilized quarters.

"Ah, very good," I said cheerfully. "Isolde, why don't you sit next to Mateo? Anubis and Ra, please stand behind the sofa."

Isolde sat down as told and looked uneasy to see Anubis and Ra standing behind her in that room.

"I have a simple question: Who are the enemies of Vlady, Nicolae, and Ilie?"

Silence.

"Who hated those three?"

"Your excellence, nobody hates anyone," said Isolde.

"Do you like Anubis and Ra?"

"Well, they are from a lower caste..."

"Who were Vlady, Nicolae, and Ilie's friends, then?"

"In that case, Lucian and Dragomir." Mateo exchanged glances with Isolde, as if making sure he said the right thing. Isolde affirmed it with a short nod.

"Therefore Tristan, Trudy, Sandor, Bogdan, Ladeena, Giselle, and Klara would be their enemies. Even you, Isolde and Mateo."

"Why would you say that?" Isolde seemed shocked.

"What would you do if Vlady, Nicolae, and Ilie, assisted by Lucian and Dragomir, were to unseat Queen Eleonore from her throne?"

"That is preposterous." Mateo rose to his feet.

"And who would be the monarch then?" Isolde asked.

"Stop asking stupid questions, Isolde," admonished Mateo.

"I will be the new queen," I said with my chin raised. I tightened my stomach muscles to control the butterflies inside me.

"A coup d'état?" Mateo asked.

"Yes. Will you be on my side, along with Vlady, Nicolae, Ilie, Lucian, Dragomir, Anubis and Ra?"

Just then, the clock on the wall banged out the half hour, and I, along with Isolde and Mateo, jumped. Ra and Anubis stood still like two statues.

"Will you be on my side, Mateo and Isolde?" I asked again.

"Pardon me, Catherina, but why would you need our allegiance?" Isolde asked.

Darn women—even if they are vampires, they always ask questions.

"Because at my court, you either are on my side or you are an enemy." That's the best I could come up with. I realized that, at present, in this room, there were only the lower members of the court. It didn't look good, but it was high noon and I had to draw.

"I'm sorry, but you have no right to do such a thing or ask us to join you." Isolde looked at Mateo, who seemed to agree with her.

Oh, well. My ace in the hole hadn't worked. They weren't convinced that Vlady, Nicolae, Ilie, Lucian, Dragomir, Anubis, and Ra were powerful enough to dethrone the queen.

"Anubis and Ra!" I shouted. "Take them away and put them someplace they cannot be heard from."

Chapter 31. Cat

This was not good. I was naive to think that Isolde and Mateo, after spending centuries with Eleonore, would change allegiances. The queen had ten vampires at her disposal. At that very moment, not counting my friends, I had two: Anubis and Ra, and three illusory traitors who were no longer alive.

I wondered where Angelique, Mundibuto, and François were. Were they able to neutralize the queen? Or were they, too, in trouble like me? I dispelled any negative thoughts. Maybe the queen was no longer a queen, and her vampires had joined my friends. Or they were dead. I shuddered.

Tudor. Where was he? I stood up and found the stairs to the first level, looking for him. The two of us could escape and distance ourselves from this castle and the queen. I arrived in a hallway full of doors on the first floor of one of the castle's wings.

"Tudor, Tudor!" I shouted. I heard a knock from a door nearby. "Tudor, are you in there?"

"Cat, I'm in here," he answered from inside.

I depressed the handle, but the door was locked. "Stand back," I told him, not sure if I could open the door without blowing it to pieces. I imagined the clicks of the lock mechanism while thinking, *unlock*. The door opened.

I ran in and jumped into Tudor's arms. "Tudor, are you OK?" I said between kisses.

"Yes, yes, but how are you?"

"Fine. Let's get out of here." I took him by the hand and we exited into the hallway.

"What happened to those terrible vampires?"

Good question. Two were, hopefully, restrained, and the other two, Anubis and Ra, were...they were my subjects. I couldn't run and leave them behind at the mercy of the queen and her vampires. They would be killed for sure.

"I have to tell you something very serious," I said. "The two terrible vampires, Anubis and Ra, are on my side. I had them incarcerate two other vampires who would not betray the queen."

"What are you saying? Actually, that's good." He smiled.

"Yes and no. I was planning a coup d'état, but only Ra and Anubis joined me."

Tudor looked at me, confused. "I don't understand. How could you overthrow the queen? How many followers do you have?"

I raised two fingers.

"Where are your other friends? Can they help you?"

"I don't know where they are or what they're doing at the moment."

"Would the queen's vampires accept your treasonous act?"

"I don't know. I am of royal blood, but I'm not a vampire."

"That's good and bad. What were you thinking?"

"My great-grandfather enjoyed good standing in the vampire community, and by being his blood, I thought I could pretend to overthrow the queen. It is not as crazy as it sounds. The army we discovered and destroyed did not belong to the queen but to Vlady, Nicolae, and Ilie, and a few other traitors of the court. The queen and the others don't know what has happened to them, and I told the vampires in the castle that they sided with me. Hopefully, with my friends' help, I could have pulled off this takeover."

Tudor stood silently, but I could see that he was churning the information in his mind. It probably sounded unbelievable to him. I was just a young woman, a human, taking on foes who could end my life with the snap of a finger.

"I don't know, Cat. It sounds very dangerous. Let's get out of here. Where is our car?"

At that moment, Ra appeared at one end of the hallway.

"Ra, do you know where Tudor's car is?"

He hesitated. "The car was given to an accomplice to take to Hungary to a chop shop," he replied. "Would you like another car?"

"Yes, please."

We followed him through other passages and ended up in an underground garage. There were several cars in there, and Tudor selected a domestic Dacia. The keys were in the ignition.

"Can you open the garage door?" I asked Ra.

"Sure, but are you leaving us?"

That was the question that was eating at me. I couldn't leave Ra and Anubis after what had happened. But Tudor didn't have to be part of this. I put my arms around him and said, "For my sake and your safety, Tudor, get away from here."

"I won't leave you. I won't leave without you."

"Please, you must. Understand that I have protection from my Strigoi. You have nothing. You are just a human who could be killed in the blink of an eye by the vampires. Please, Tudor. Leave."

He shook his head.

"You must leave." I swallowed hard and repeated in a stronger tone. "You must leave. Now."

He kept shaking his head.

"Men—you are all alike. Do as your head tells you, not as your heart tells you."

"I'll never leave you." He caressed my hair.

"Tudor, listen. We had a fling. A good fling, but now it must end. It was going to end anyway when we went back to Timisoara."

He froze and then whispered, "I thought that you...I love you. Don't you love me?"

"I like you," I said with a cold stare. "That was all there was between us."

He lowered his arms, defeated.

"Ra, open the garage door. The doctor is leaving us."

Ra complied, opening the door and letting in the dawn light.

"Leave." I pointed to the exit.

Tudor looked at me with sad eyes. But he slowly got in the car, started the engine, and drove off.

Chapter 32. Cat

I covered my face with my hands and cried. Tudor was such a sweet man, and in the short time we had spent together, I had fallen in love with him. But I would rather not have him than see him killed. And who knew? If I were to come out of this alive, there was always hope that I would see him again.

Ra stood with his arms crossed, waiting for me. I wiped my face with my hands and considered the situation the two vampires and I were in. The queen may or may not return. I hoped that my friends had succeeded or at least had come to an agreement with her. Most likely they hadn't, and she would return with her vampires. And what about my friends? I didn't want to think about that. I had to prepare for the worst.

"Where is Anubis?" I asked Ra.

"In the dungeons, locking Mateo and Isolde in a secret place they cannot leave."

"Good. Take me there."

Ra led me through more underground passages to a deep pit in the ground. Anubis was placing a heavy iron grate on it.

"Are they in there?" I asked.

"Yes, Catherina," answered Anubis.

"It is a deep and silent place. How long will they stay there?" Ra asked.

"Until this is over."

"What would you have us do, Catherina?" Ra asked.

"Tell me—when a vampire doesn't please the queen, what does she do with him or her?"

"He is placed in an iron box," answered Ra.

"Iron box?"

"I'll show you." Ra invited me to follow him to another dungeon. Anubis followed as well, and we arrived in a stone cell with several iron boxes the size of super-large caskets. There were six of them aligned against the wall.

"What are those?"

Without answering, Ra opened the lid of one of them by turning a wheel as if opening a vault door. The rectangular box had two-inch-thick steel walls. The steel door was even thicker and its locking mechanism had latching rods all around the perimeter, just like a safe.

"The vampire is placed in here, locked up, and held until the queen decides on a verdict."

"Have you been locked in one of these?"

Anubis and Ra nodded.

"It is impossible to escape once you're placed inside one of these," said Ra.

"That's where you placed Mateo and Isolde?"

"Yes, but deep inside that pit."

"Are they going to be OK in them?"

"A vampire can stay in one of these boxes for a long time," said Anubis.

Boxes specifically made for restraining vampires. I shivered about what I needed to do next.

"Anubis and Ra, you have to understand that, if things don't go as planned, you may end up in one of these boxes."

They looked at each other, uneasy.

"But you have everything planned, right?" said Ra.

Assurances were mandatory. "Of course. And to prevent you from ending up in one of the boxes, you must be temporarily enclosed in them."

Both of them looked at me, stunned.

"Why?" Anubis asked.

"For your protection."

"Don't understand," said Anubis.

"Listen carefully. This is a possibility. The queen will come back and she'll find just the three of us in the castle, with Mateo and Isolde missing. Tudor has escaped. What do you think will happen?"

They were not the sharpest vampires in this dungeon. They stared at me, blankly.

"The queen will question you and me," I said. "One of us will talk, and then we'll all be in trouble. We would end up in those boxes for sure."

"But your subjects will be here to do battle and to defend you. And us," said Ra.

"That's correct, but just in case they are late, I have a plan."

"I don't know," said Ra, scratching the feathers on his head. "Anubis, we'd better let Isolde and Mateo out. This was a mistake."

"There was no mistake. If you let the other two out, they will tell the queen, and you'll end up in the boxes anyway."

"That's true," said Anubis.

"However, when the queen comes back and I were the only one in the castle, she will have only me to question. I will tell her that I commanded my Strigoi to put you in the boxes, that I liberated Tudor, and that Mateo and Isolde are my subjects and went away to call Vlady, Nicolae, and Ilie, along with the proto-vampires, to my aid."

"Proto-vampires?" Ra asked.

"Yes, you don't think that I came here to take over the kingdom of vampires just on the basis of my royal blood line?"

Anubis and Ra shook their heads but seemed to be encouraged by the news.

"You see now? If I imprison you, the queen will not suspect you of treason. You'll be safe that way, while my subjects and proto-vampires take over the castle."

Without a word, Anubis and Ra opened the lids and stepped inside. Anubis lay down, crossing his arms over his chest.

Ra seemed reluctant. "You are a human. You cannot put us in the boxes by force."

170

He wasn't as dumb as I thought. "Good point, Ra," I said, thinking of a good way to give the impression that I had forced them into the boxes, and then it came to me. "I levitated you."

"What's that?" asked Anubis, as he rose halfway up from his box.

"Floated you in the air. Like this." I extended my hand and I imagined the box Anubis was in rising above the floor. The box rose a few feet. Anubis panicked, and I placed the box back on the ground before he could cling onto the ceiling.

The two vampires stared at me and without a word, each of them lay down in his box. I motioned with my hand, and the lids closed on them. I turned the wheels and they were imprisoned, but safe.

Chapter 33. Cat

I was alone in the castle. This place was a museum, and tourists would come to visit during regular hours, so I had to find a place to hide. I was tired and needed some sleep. The bedroom with the bathroom I was in earlier was a functioning bedroom, so it must not be open to tourists. I decided to retire to that room until it was dark or until the queen returned.

It was dusk when I woke up. The museum-castle was already closed for business, and it was quiet, like any other museum at night. I was starving, so I decided to find some food. Vampires don't eat food; they only drink human blood for their life sustenance and alcohol for their energy. Either liquid was out of the question for me, but Anubis had brought food to Tudor. I went to the room he had previously occupied and inside I found several unopened cans of stew. They would have to do.

I wandered through the castle while debating where to wait for the queen. The throne room was elaborately furnished with medieval fittings. It was the room with the four bay windows providing a breathtaking view over the evening lights outside. Red velvet, carpeted steps led up to the golden throne. It was a modern replica but very comfortable when I sat in it. This was a good place to play my part and to make myself comfortable in the meanwhile—too comfortable, as it turned out, because I dozed off.

"Who the hell are you?" A sharp voice woke me up.

A brunette—a vampire, no doubt—in a dusty, ripped red velvet jacket and tall leather boots stood in front of the throne I was sprawled on. She stared at me, with her hands on her hips.

It took me a minute to recover my wits. "I am Princess Catherina of the Draculesti family. And who the hell are *you*?"

She was taken aback. "Princess?"

"Yes. Where is Queen Eleonore? Is she back yet? What is your name?" The best way to keep people on their toes is to ask questions.

She seemed at a loss for words.

"Your name? You do have a name, don't you?" I demanded.

"Lady-in-waiting Giselle, your excellence." And she curtsied, which was a good start. "Does her majesty know about you?"

"Where is Eleonore, Giselle? Go fetch her." I shooed her away with my hand. And she went.

From across the throne room a loud high-pitched voice asked, "Princess who? Get out of my way, I've got to see this." Eleonore, guessing by her voice, came into the room at an un-queenly trot and didn't stop until she reached the steps below the throne. Her eyes just about popped out of her sockets. "What's the meaning of this?"

I sat on the throne with my legs crossed, looking down my nose at her. "Do you know who I am, Eleonore?"

Giselle and another dame, dressed similarly, came running after her. "How dare you address Queen Eleonore by her first name?" the other one said in a huff, holding her arm as if she were injured.

"Guards, guards!" Giselle screamed at the top of her lungs.

One big hulk of a vampire followed by another smaller, limping vampire rushed inside. The big one had weapons on him.

"Stop shouting!" Eleonore looked over her shoulder and barked orders, "Dragomir, Bogdan, bring the strong boxes into the main under-chamber. Giselle and Klara go and take care of the injured." She turned and looked at me with mean eyes. "Cat. Who in hell gave you permission to sit on my throne?"

"What took you so long to return?"

"Get down from there, or do you want me to yank you by your hair down onto your knees?"

One thing I didn't want was for her to grab me. It was time to descend gracefully. I rose up in the air, floated, and landed behind her. My Strigoi did that.

"Your damn Strigoi," she hissed.

I smiled airily at her.

"What did you tell Giselle your name was?"

"Princess Catherina of the Draculesti family."

Eleonore was not a particularly good-looking woman in her sick years before Vlad took pity on her and changed her into a vampire, but now, after hearing my title and name, she looked like the grim reaper.

"You are going to be very sorry, missy." She spat the words out at me.

"'Your excellence' will do," I replied cheekily.

"If you think that I'm impressed by your ancestors, think again. Besides, since that pain in the ass great-grandfather of yours is dead, I'm the ultimate power in the vampire world. Pray that I let you live."

"Why did you kidnap me?" I asked her.

She didn't answer me. "I have a lot of questions for you. Since you arrived here, suspicious things have happened. I think you have something to do with them."

Klara approached and curtsied. "Your majesty, we brought everything into the main under-chamber, and we are ready for you."

"Has anyone died yet?" she asked.

"Good news—they are all alive, your majesty. By the way, the police are at the back door of the second safe house."

My spirits lifted. The police were coming to rescue me.

"What do they want?"

"They brought back the man who was with her." Klara motioned toward me.

"Tudor?"

Chapter 34. Cat

"The police have Dr. Lupu? He escaped?" Eleonore looked at me with a mixture of surprise and a bad case of indigestion.

"I believe so," Klara said.

"Where are Mateo and Isolde?"

"They are nowhere to be found, your majesty."

"Where are the mutants Ra and Anubis?"

"They are missing, too, your majesty."

"What the hell did you do while I was away?" Eleonore asked me with exasperation in her voice.

"I let Dr. Lupu go," I replied with dread.

"Like hell you did," said the queen. "Klara, stay with her and contact me if she makes any wrong moves. I'll go take possession of the doctor to tame this little pain in the ass."

Klara moved in front of me and adjusted her walkie-talkie on her belt as a warning.

Instead of staying away, Tudor decided to go to the police and ask for help. Unfortunately, he contacted the wrong officers, the ones who were on Eleonore's payroll. This was a major setback, but I'd deal with it.

"So, you're Klara?" I asked.

"I'm Lady Klara to you," she answered defiantly.

"That's right. That's what Isolde and Ladeena insisted on being called. Where is Ladeena?" I asked.

"Where is Isolde?" she asked.

I shrugged.

"Why are you asking for Ladeena?"

"Why are you in such deplorable condition?" I looked at Klara's clothes, which were not only dirty but had holes in them. She held her right arm close to her chest. "Are those bullet holes?"

"Maybe."

"Oh, poor dear. What happened to you? Are you OK?" I did my best to show concern for her condition. That seemed to soften her a little.

"Those damn vampires ambushed us."

Was she talking about Angelique, Mundibuto, and François? "Which vampires do you mean?"

"Come to think of it, they are your friends."

"Who?" I had to be sure.

"François, Angelique, and that black vampire, Mundibuto."

"What did you do to them?" I was really worried.

"It's not what we did to them, it's what we will do to them."

"What?"

"Do you see these holes?" She pointed to the holes on her sleeve and her pants' legs. "These were caused by your friends. And you know what that bitch Angelique did to Ladeena? She blinded her. Do I have to give you more details of what we will do to them after what they did to us?"

"Where are my friends?"

"We got them. And they'll wish they were never born after we're done with them."

"Where do you have them?" I imagined them in chains in iron-barred cages.

"We have them good and tight in the main under-chamber."

"I don't believe you. Take me there to see them."

"Hell! Not a chance."

"Good, then I'll go and find them myself."

She planted her feet as if ready to defend a charge. I glided to the right. She jumped quickly in front of me. I moved faster to the left. She leaped to face me but she was slower. I began moving in random patterns on the floor, compliments of my Strigoi, but Klara, although a vampire, couldn't keep track of me, and I ended up behind her. I already had my lipstick out of my pocket, and I pressed it to the back of her neck.

"Even vampires die from bullets." I pressed the tube harder on her neck to leave the impression of the tube and then glided back.

Klara might have been sluggish from her wounds but not sluggish enough not to turn and try to grab my hand before I could even see it happening. She turned in the blink of an eye, but her hand grabbed nothing but air. I was already out of her reach.

"You're not fast enough. Do you want to play again, or do you want to lead me to the main under-chamber?" I unscrewed the lipstick and applied some to my lips.

She looked shaken. No human could have moved faster than a vampire, but I did with some anticipation and the help of my Strigoi. She saw the powers I possessed and was considering her options. She pulled her walkie-talkie from her belt and blurted out, "Your majesty, Catherina insists to be taken to the main under-chamber. Should I do that?"

After some crackling static, the queen answered, "Might as well. That's where we're going to be."

Klara seemed relieved that she could escort me to that room. "I'm keeping an eye on you. No funny business on the way there."

"I promise. Lead on."

She walked in front of me, halfway turned, keeping an eye on me. I followed her to a fake door in the wall from where we took a long spiral brick stairway down. We ended up in a chamber identical to the throne room above. Four niches, closed up by iron bars, replaced the four bay windows that made the throne room so large and airy just a few stories above. This was the real vampire throne room, where all the horrors took place.

The room looked like a hospital triage center. It was lined with cots where moaning vampires lay. It looked as if these vampires had come from a war. As far as I could tell, all the male vampires were wounded, except perhaps for Dragomir. Giselle and Ruxandra were attending to the wounded but could hardly do anything more than comfort them. Painkillers or any other medication would not help vampires. They had a different physiology, and they had to heal by themselves even when in pain. I was able to recognize some of them and deduce who the others were.

On one of the cots I saw Ladeena. She had a bandage around her eyes. Where her eye sockets were the bandage was a sickly blue. She was holding her chest, and through her fingers I spotted many bullet holes in her jacket, just as some of the other vampires had.

I wanted to ask who had done that to them, but I knew who the culprits were. My friends. I shivered, imagining what might have happened.

"Where are my friends?" I asked Klara.

Giselle, Ruxandra, and the vampires who were conscious turned their eyes toward me, surprised and shocked that I was there.

"There." Klara pointed to three big steel boxes on the floor.

Chapter 35. Cat

They were kept in boxes similar to the ones I had placed Ra and Anubis in. I hoped my friends were well. I walked closer to the boxes.

"Stop!" a voice shouted from behind me. "Don't let her get closer to those boxes."

I turned and saw Eleonore. Behind her, Dragomir held Tudor by the arm, pulling him in. I ran to him, but Dragomir's hand stopped me.

"Put him in one of those cages." Eleonore pointed to one of the niches with the heavy bars on them.

Dragomir moved Tudor with ease and threw him into the far right cell, after which he slammed the door and locked it. I followed them and after Tudor was inside, I grabbed the bars and cried, seeing him on the floor, trying slowly to get up.

"Tudor, are you hurt?"

"I'm fine, Cat." He came close to the bars and placed his hands over mine.

"Hey, get away from the bars!" Dragomir hollered.

I gave him a murderous glare.

"Let them be," said the queen. "Let her see what's she's risking, if she misbehaves."

"Tudor, why didn't you go away like I told you to?" I asked.

"I'm sorry. I couldn't abandon you. I went to the police, who took me with them to confirm my complaint, but instead they delivered me back to the queen." He shook his head, disappointed.

"I'll get us out of here," I whispered.

A loud bang sounded behind me. Dragomir, Giselle, Klara, and Ruxandra dropped onto the floor three rusty steel contraptions, which they had brought from somewhere deeper underground. They lifted each device and placed them upright on the nearby wall, after which they locked them with heavy bolts. Each of the contraptions was a steel structure in an "X" shape, and each had heavy shackles at the extremities. Once installed, Dragomir pulled from a recessed electrical panel heavy insulated cables and attached two each on each X structure, one at the top and the other at the bottom. He was planning an electrocution.

My blood pressure sank. Those contrivances were electrical torturing devices. But on whom would they use them? Not my friends, I hoped.

"What are those, Eleonore?"

She and her subjects had given up admonishing me for not addressing her with respect.

"What do they look like? Electrocution racks. Aren't they ingenious?" She looked at me all excited, as if showing me the greatest gadget in the world.

Some of the vampires laughed with anticipation of what was about to happen.

The queen looked at me, pleased to see me in shock. "There is one for each of your friends."

"You don't have to do this," I pleaded.

"You're right, I don't have to do this." With a sneer, she added, "I want to and I'll enjoy each and every scream coming out of their mouths."

"Why do this?"

"For a variety of reasons, which you'll learn in due time. Let me ask you again—where are Isolde, Mateo, Ra, and Anubis?"

She had Tudor. She had my friends in steel boxes, and she was planning to electrocute them.

The time was right to lie and extract some concessions in return. "I'll tell you, but only if you promise not to hurt Dr. Lupu and my friends."

"You are in no position to bargain. Bogdan would love to suck the last drop of blood from Dr. Lupu."

As if to make her point, Bogdan limped to the cage where Tudor was, licking his lips. Tudor backed up against the brick wall, horrified.

"Stay where you are!" I screamed at Bogdan. "OK, Eleonore, you win, but you may not like what I'll tell you."

"I'm all ears," she said.

"Isolde and Mateo ran away."

Eleonore burst out laughing.

"Seriously, they told me that they would join Vlady, Nicolae, and Ilie in a rebellion against you."

"What?" she shrieked.

Lucian sat up, concerned. Dragomir moved menacingly closer to me.

"Is this the first time you've heard of this?" I shook my head, pitying her.

"What rebellion?" Eleonore advanced toward me, eyes on fire.

"And they are not alone."

"Who else is with them?"

"I met Vlady and the other two vampires in Sighisoara. They told me and showed me their army of zombies—"

"Bullshit!" Lucian shouted, getting up from his cot.

"And proto-vampires."

Eleonore stood a few feet away from me, stunned with disbelief. "What is all this talk about proto-vampires?" She raised her hands, confused.

"Sorry to be the messenger of bad news," I said.

"You're lying." She shook a finger at me. "You are lying."

"If I'm not telling the truth, where are they now? All five of them?"

"Why did they tell you about their rebellion and show you the army?"

"To convince me to join them," I whispered confidentially.

"Convince you to join them for what purpose?"

"I am of royal blood, and they want me to be the new queen of vampires."

Chapter 36. Cat

The next thing I knew, she was holding me up by my throat, letting my feet dangle. Eleonore looked at me with so much hatred that I was afraid she would kill me right there and then. My lungs were on fire, and my neck felt as if it were in a vise. I couldn't even summon my Strigoi.

She unclenched her hand and let me drop. Standing over me, she spat at me and then kicked me, rolling me on the floor like a ragdoll. Luckily, I didn't lose consciousness, and although hurt from her kicks to my ribs and hips, I stood up shakily. My throat was throbbing and I wasn't sure if I could talk.

"Royal blood, huh?" she screamed. "That's what pretend royal blood gets, a kick in the ass, for starters. Let's see how much royal blood you have when you witness the slow and agonizing deaths of your friends." She accentuated every word with a pointed finger at me. She motioned with her head. "Let's get them out of the boxes."

I staggered away.

"Giselle, hold her by the back of the neck," she ordered. "Don't let her get away, and make sure she sees what will happen next." She snapped her fingers. "Dragomir and Bogdan, turn on the juice."

I wasn't sure what she meant, but to my horror Dragomir pulled a pair of electric cables from the electric panel and, using clamps, he attached one cable to each end of a box. Oh my God! They were going to electrocute them in the boxes! I placed both of my hands over my mouth.

"Give it a jolt," she ordered, while placing her hands on her hips.

Bogdan pushed up a blade switch on the electrical panel. The switch sparked, and I could hear the electricity buzzing. It felt as if Bogdan held the switch up for an eternity, but he pulled it down after a few seconds, disconnecting the electricity, while blue sparks flew out of the copper blades.

Dragomir approached the strong box, spun the locking wheel, and threw open the lid. He reached into the box and pulled a limp François out, holding him in a bear hug. He then took him to the nearest X-cross and, together with Bogdan, shackled him onto the cross.

A few seconds later, François lifted his head and focused on the room around him, expressionless. He was restrained at the wrists and elbows, around the waist, at the ankles and above the knees with heavy steel shackles that even a vampire could not break.

"Next!" Eleonore ordered.

After the cables were connected to the next box, Bogdan pushed the switch up and repeated the procedure. Dragomir quickly opened the lid, but this time a handgun fired from inside, hitting Dragomir on the side of his shoulder before he could slam the lid down. He didn't suffer a disabling wound; the bullet just grazed his arm and tore his sleeve.

"Zap him again!" Dragomir yelled, and Bogdan pushed up the switch again, administering another jolt.

Dragomir opened the box and pulled out a wilted Mundibuto, took him to another X-cross, and shackled him onto it. He punched Mundibuto in the head. Mundibuto woke up and looked around, disoriented. Dragomir cursed and punched him in the stomach for good measure.

"Angelique the bitch is last," said Eleonore. "Give her a smaller jolt, Bogdan. I don't want her dead. Yet."

I wasn't sure how much smaller a jolt she got, but when Dragomir pulled her out of the box, she was unconscious. She ended up on an X-cross like the others and did not regained consciousness as quickly as the men. Even after she raised her head, she looked dazed.

"Excellent." Eleonore clasped her hands together as if admiring a great work of art. "As you see, Catherina-the-wanna-be-queen, your vampire friends are immobilized and at my disposal. Vampires are strong, but they are not stronger than electricity, because, you know, of the copper in our blood. Vampire bodies conduct electricity more efficiently, and they feel the full jolt of the electrons rushing through them." She smiled maliciously. "It is time to tell me more about the rebellion, or I will zap them again until you talk or they die."

I didn't have much choice, and frankly I hadn't expected this to happen. It was foolish of me to think that the queen would crawl into a hole and that the rest of the vampires would rally to my side. I had to tell my most believable lies and see if I could find a way out of this. I hoped.

To me, it seemed that Vlady, Ilie, and Nicolae had been plotting something by having an army of zombies and proto-vampires. Not even Eleonore envisioned the creation of proto-vampires, but those three and other traitors did. I was almost sure the other traitors were Dragomir and Lucian. Of the two, Dragomir was in good shape. Lucian was awake, partly recovered and staring at me nervously.

The fact that I mentioned the proto-vampires assured them of my knowledge of their army. Did they know that Mundibuto, Tudor, and I had destroyed it, turning it into dust? Maybe Dragomir or Lucian hadn't had enough time to visit Sighisoara and find out what had happened. I didn't think they knew about the disaster we had left behind.

Vlady, Ilie, and Nicolae had left Tudor and me locked in the suspended cages under the cemetery for a good amount of time to consult with someone about what to do with me. Tudor was irrelevant to their machinations. But Vlad's ashes, which turned into a luminescent cloud, and I were of concern to them. Why did they tell me that the army was the queen's army? How much did they divulge to Dragomir, who seemed nervous at this moment, and Lucian even more so. What would they do to me this time if I told the truth? I had to find the answers to these questions and other information during Eleonore's interrogation of me.

"Well, what are you waiting for?" she demanded.

"First, would you tell Giselle to stop gripping the back of my neck so hard? I'm not a vampire. I'm getting a headache, and I can't concentrate."

Eleonore made a small motion with her head, and Giselle relaxed her grip. A bit.

I sighed. "What do you want to know?"

"Everything."

"Everything? Well then, you must want to know what happened to Ra and Anubis."

Chapter 37. Cat

"What happened to Ra and Anubis?" she asked worriedly.

I needed to gain time for my vampire friends to recover from the electric shocks, and then I would attempt to free them with my Strigoi's help. It was worth trying.

"Well, Isolde and Ladeena became agitated and placed me in a cell next to Dr. Lupu."

"Yes, I know that, and I told Isolde to free you, and then what?"

"After Isolde and Mateo left, I went to the dungeon and demanded Dr. Lupu's release. Anubis refused, and I used my Strigoi to levitate him."

"You what?"

"I suspended him in midair."

"Yes, I know what that means," she said impatiently.

"Can she do that?" Giselle asked from behind me.

"That and more," I replied. I felt Giselle's grip tremble.

Eleonore crossed her arms. She looked unsure about what she had heard. "And then what did you do with him?"

"I took him to one of those strong boxes and shoved him in one of them. And I locked it." I made a motion with my hand as if turning a wheel. "I did the same thing to Ra. They are both in the strong boxes."

"How did you know about the strong boxes?"

"Nicolae told me about them and where they were." I stopped talking to let my incredible lie sink in.

"Klara, Ruxandra, go get Ra and Anubis out," she ordered. "Enough of this. What did you do with Isolde and Mateo?"

"Isolde and Ladeena became agitated and placed me in a cell."

"You already said that." She sensed that I was dragging my feet.

"After Ladeena left, Isolde freed me. And after that, I asked for her cell phone and I called Nicolae and I told him what happened."

"You called Nicolae." I could see Eleonore's jaw muscles tensing.

"Yes, and he asked me to put Isolde on the phone, and next thing I know, she and Mateo are fleeing the castle to join him. I think that's what they did."

"How did you know Mateo?"

"He brought my luggage from the car. That's when I met him. He kissed my hand." That lie was a good one, as kissing a lady's hand in Europe was a sign of respect, at least it was in the past. Eleonore's reaction reaffirmed what I expected: Mateo had looked up to me as a royal princess.

"Goddamn you." She paced around, while the rest held their breath in anticipation of hearing what was next. "What did they take with them?"

I shrugged. "It was dark when they fled."

"And then you let him go?" She pointed to Tudor.

"Yes. I asked him to get away from all this vampire mess."

"When did you find out about this plot?"

"I was told about it by my great-great-grandfather Vlad, back in New York."

"That son of a bitch. He was behind all this. What did he tell you to do?"

"Before he died, he told me that a forward-looking group of vampires was paving the way for me to take my rightful place as the queen of vampires."

"I'm going to kill you. Oh, I'm so going to kill you and those bastards." She pointed a shaking finger at my friends. "I'm going to pull Vlady's tongue out." She was furious, curling her fingers as to rip someone apart. "Did you know Nicolae, Vlady, or Ilie before you came to Transylvania?"

"No. My great-grandfather told me to go to Sighisoara and spread his ashes from the tower. That would give the signal for the rebellion to start." I noticed Dragomir blinking and Lucian standing with his fists clenched. I wondered if I was saying too much, but at that moment Klara and Ruxandra came in with Anubis and Ra.

"There you are, you worthless chicken shits."

Terrified, Ra and Anubis trembled visibly.

She asked Klara and Ruxandra, "Where did you find them?"

"Just like she said, in the strong boxes, your majesty," replied Ruxandra.

"How the hell did you get in those boxes, you miserable creatures?"

"She floated us in the air," said Ra, looking around the room and seeming not to like what he was seeing.

"Yes, in the air," said Anubis, and his ears flicked nervously.

"Then she shoved us in the boxes," concluded Ra.

"Did you see Isolde and Mateo running away?"

They hesitated and then shook their heads. That was good: The less they said, the less trouble they'd have with the queen.

"I'll deal with you later. Help Klara and Ruxandra." She turned to me and seemed to be concerned about what I could possibly be capable of doing to her or her vampires. "Bogdan, give them some juice, as they say in America, to loosen her tongue some more."

"Gladly." Bogdan walked across the room with less of a limp than before. He was healing, and it wouldn't be long before he would be back at his full strength again. He opened another control panel, and in the middle of it was a large black knob with an arrow pointing at zero on a scale up to 4,000. "How many volts, my queen?" He sneered.

"Give them 1,000 volts," she said, jutting her chin.

"No!" protested Angelique from the cross.

Bogdan moved the big knob and stopped when the arrow pointed to 1,000 V.

My vampire friends tensed up as the current flowed through them, from one hand to the opposite ankle. All their muscles contracted from the stress caused by the electricity.

"Enough!" I shouted.

Chapter 38. Cat

Eleonore motioned to Bogdan to stop. He turned the knob to zero. My vampire friends slumped on their X-crosses, breathing heavily. The ghastly sight made me dizzy with fear and horror.

"Tell me more," the queen invited me to continue.

"I'll tell you everything. You don't have to torture them," I pleaded.

"Of course you will. Go on, spill the beans."

"They have collaborators in your court," I said in a trembling voice.

"Who are they?"

I looked around the room. Dragomir and Lucian were tense. The other vampires—by now they were all paying attention, except for Ladeena, who couldn't see—seemed to be innocent, watching each other with fearful curiosity.

"Isn't it obvious?" I asked. "Who went looking for Vlady, Ilie, and Nicolae after they went missing?"

"Say again?" Her head turned quickly, fixing Bogdan with her stare.

The vampire trembled and blinked rapidly with fear.

"Bogdan and Sandor, I sent you to find them after Vlady disposed of Mundibuto. You told me that they disappeared without a trace."

"They did, your majesty," said a trembling Bogdan from the control panel.

"We didn't find them anywhere, your majesty." Sandor raised his hand from his cot as if he were swearing an oath.

"Who told you that they had disposed of me?" Mundibuto laughed. Everyone looked at him on the cross.

"I asked you how you got out of your rat hole, and you told me you climbed out!" Eleonore screamed at him.

"We told you what you wanted to hear," he answered.

"We?"

"Nicolae, Ilie, and Vlady—my buddies." Mundibuto smiled at her. He had caught onto my lie, and he was playing along.

"You are in the clique with them," Eleonore said with relief, as if seeing the whole plot unfurl before her eyes.

Indeed, Bogdan and Sandor were not accomplices. That left Tristan and Trudy to be tested. Angelique looked at me, and I motioned with my eyes to Tristan and Trudy. She understood.

"They're all in the clique with them, Eleonore," said Angelique. "Like the one with the wounded arm and the one holding his stomach."

"How dare you!" shouted Trudy. "Your majesty, I'm your trusted valet. She's lying."

Tristan sat up with great effort. "Don't believe those lies. I've been your secretary for over 300 years."

"You're also Isolde's brother," sneered Eleonore, raising her arms in dismay. She yelled at the top of her lungs, pacing around. "I'm surrounded by traitors! Traitors! All of you!"

There was dead silence in the hall. I felt better that I didn't have to help anymore. The fire had been ignited, and it was going to consume them all.

"Your majesty, what would you wish me to do?" asked Lucian, but she ignored him.

"How about you, Dragomir?" the queen asked. "How would you punish the traitors?"

"Behead them all," Dragomir said without hesitation.

François caught my eye. He made me look in the direction of the electrical control panel. I didn't know what I was looking at. There was a bunch of green, red, and black round pushbuttons; a small round green light; the knob with the arrow; and on the upper right side, a yellow lever similar to the one Bogdan had used to zap my friends when they were in the strong boxes. I realized what François wanted me to do: Pull that lever down using my Strigoi. I blinked my eyes in acknowledgment, assuring him that I knew what needed to be done.

"Behead them all?" asked Queen Eleonore rhetorically. "Good advice. Lucian, bring me my sword."

"Your majesty, please," several plaintive voices called to her.

I used this opportunity, while every one was pleading and begging, to concentrate on the lever, and click—my Strigoi pushed it down. The green light on the panel went out. At least for the moment, the electricity was off.

"Silence!" Eleonore roared. "The true at heart will survive. Only the guilty will be punished. Ra, Anubis—bring me the impaling shaft."

That didn't sound good. What in hell was she planning now?

It didn't take long for the two vampires to bring in a contraption that belonged in a museum of torture. It was a rack with a sharp steel rod, blackened by old blood and as thick as a man's forearm. It left no doubt what it was used for: *impaling*.

"Do I need to tell you what that is?" Eleonore looked mischievously at me.

I shook my head. There was no need for much imagination to feel the pain that the sharp rod would inflict on its victim.

"And the reason I brought it out," Eleonore spoke to everyone, "although I haven't used it in ages, is to impale someone. Just like your great-great-granduncle, Vlad the Impaler, used to do." She smiled at me. "I admired him for his ability to control by fear, although I never met him. He was a master at inflicting pain and suffering." She cackled with delight. "And that's what I'll do next."

It was not possible. She would impale one of her vampires? I felt nauseated.

Limping, Lucian approached her, holding a sheathed samurai sword, which she pulled out and rested on her shoulder. The steel gleamed with cold intent.

"The problem with the darn impaling rod is that it is not good against vampires," Eleonore continued. "The steel will rust before a vampire will die. That's why beheading is the best way to punish traitors."

Her sword slashed out with such speed that, at first, I thought she was just exercising her sword for effect. Then I heard a gasp from the vampires.

A split second later, Lucian head toppled from this body.

Chapter 39. Cat

Lucian's body stood upright. Eleonore kicked it, and it collapsed, convulsing violently. Blue blood covered the blade of her sword. She impaled the head through the neck and raised Lucian's head high in the air for everyone to see. His eyes blinked several times. He even moved them and focused on me before closing them. His brain was still alive but not for long.

"Long live our queen!" shouted Dragomir.

"Long live our queen!" exploded from every vampire's mouth. And they repeated the shout two more times.

Queen Eleonore paced calmly around Lucian's jerking body, holding the head speared on the sword. "You see, dear Catherina, the true traitor got the right punishment." She placed a boot on Lucian's twitching body and smiled at me, after which she dropped the head, which rolled in circles until it rested against his corpse. Dragomir caught the sword when she threw it to him for cleaning.

I was confused as to how she had come to her conclusion. Sure, I wanted to implicate Dragomir and Lucian as traitors against her, but she killed only Lucian. Dragomir was cleaning her sword with a satisfied smirk.

"My dear, dear Catherina," she said with a nauseating smile. "I've been the queen of vampires for over a century and a vampire for much longer. During that time, I've learned a trick or two about keeping my loyal subjects loyal. When you implied that there were traitors at my court, you were right, but there was only one traitor. Him." She kicked Lucian's corpse with disgust.

"Good, then I was right," I managed to say.

"Right for the wrong reason." The queen chuckled. "I don't know if you knew it or not, but the zombie and proto-vampire army under the cemetery in Sighisoara was mine. Vlady was in charge of it. Nicolae and Ilie were his soldiers. One day, it occurred to me that he who was in charge of the proto-vampires would reign. I needed someone smart to be the general of my army, and Vlady proved himself loyal.

"Nicolae and Ilie were two thugs. Ilie had improved over the centuries, but Nicolae was not leadership material. They wouldn't be able to think of a clever plan to commit treason against me. Everyone else was incapable of or too loyal for treason, except for two other vampires: Dragomir and Lucian. Those two were smart and they were leaders, and I had to make sure they were loyal to me. I asked Vlady to tell Dragomir and Lucian, separately, that he had a zombie and proto-vampire army, and that he was planning to overthrow me.

"Do you know what happened? I'll tell you what happened. Dragomir came to me and warned me about what Vlady had told him. However, Lucian did not. He asked Vlady to show him the army, and Vlady obliged. From that point on, Lucian thought he was conspiring with Vlady, Nicolae, and Ilie against me. His days were numbered, and they ended today." Eleonore spat on Lucian's corpse.

This was getting complicated, and I needed time to think. "Why did you create the army?" I asked, hoping to delay whatever she planned to do next.

She nodded and raised a finger as if to say, good question. "There were two reasons, my dear. First, your great-grandfather Vlad was an idealistic fool. He had noble ideas about staying out of human affairs, keeping a low profile, and enjoying life. However, vampires are superior to humans in every aspect. We live forever, as long as we have human blood. We are stronger and faster. And we are smarter. Long life is conducive to becoming smarter and wiser. That's true for most vampires—most, but not all. Therefore, why not rule the world?"

"Don't be ridiculous. Vampires may be superior, but humans number in the billions. They'll obliterate you."

"Yes, if they find out what we are and who we are. But we can rule the world from the shadows, using our puppets. And you're right—humans number in the billions. It doesn't take a genius to figure out that this planet is drowning in human filth. Not to mention that all of them claim to be equal, to have equal rights. Rights, my ass. The rule of the master and the slave will be restored. But they're too many of them, so some culling will be necessary." She shrugged. "Annihilate a few billion of them, and all will be well."

"You're mad!" I exploded.

"Wait until I tell you how it's going to be done. I doubt that you know about the cave in the Carpathians where I warehouse—sorry, where I warehoused—several thousand zombies. Thanks to your friends here, they were all set on fire. But that's just a small drawback. Humans die every day. There is no shortage of corpses to transform into zombies."

"But why zombies?"

"The zombies are created from dead people. They can be stored compactly and for very long periods of time. When needed, I awaken them and send them to create mayhem. There is a problem with them, though: They are not smart. 'Brain dead' is a more precise term. When released to attack, they act like locusts and devour all the slow living things, but not the vegetation and the quick creatures. My plan is to establish such zombie warehouses under most cemeteries. People die, they are buried, and we take the bodies and recycle them into zombies. Simple and beautiful, isn't it?"

She placed her hands behind her back and continued, "We're going to unleash them against humanity. Just like in the movies. No need for an infectious disease, guns and bullets, or nerve gas—just millions of zombies descending on the most crowded or undesirable places on Earth. And yes, the zombies are contagious. Once they bite you, you die and become a zombie. Sure, humanity is going to eradicate them once they realize what is happening. But by then, the humans would be half as many in number." She took a moment to let me absorb what she had just said. "Am I not a genius, Cat?"

"My God! You are one mad creature from hell." I shook my head in disgust.

"No, I am a vampire who thinks clearly. Thanks to Dr. Hellinherr Sr., and without him realizing what he had discovered, I am able to convert corpses into zombies and live humans into proto-vampires. The proto-vampires are stronger than humans, but not as strong as the vampires. They are intelligent and mostly obedient. The problem with them is that they need nourishment, meat and blood, and they age. Under the cemetery in Sighisoara, we experimented with keeping the proto-vampires in hibernation. When needed, we would wake them up and unleash them like soldiers to do our bidding."

"And kill more people?"

"No, zombies will do that. But someone has to lead the zombies. Why use vampires when proto-vampires can take care of the task? But there is more. In the cave where I warehoused the zombies, I'm holding twelve sarcophagi containing the bodies of, guess who?"

"The devils!" I blurted out.

"Excellent! Vlad must have told you about the one he found. There are twelve devils in there. The religions of the world talk about them because they were once real. And they will become real again. When that day comes, even vampires won't be able to fight them. I need an army of proto-vampires and zombies to protect me and my vampires from those aliens. By the way, I was about to move the proto-vampires and zombies from Sighisoara to the cave."

She viewed me quizzically.

"And now the question I have for you is, what exactly have you and your three friends come here to do? I need answers, and I would like to have fun while the truth pours out of you."

Queen Eleonore looked amused, as if she were about to surprise me. I hated to think what she had in her sick mind.

"As I said, the impaling rod doesn't work on vampires. But it works great on humans. The other human," she pointed to Tudor, "has no value to me except to make you do what I want. Talk."

I felt like fainting. She was planning to impale Tudor.

"Anubis and Ra, place the good doctor on the impaling rack."

Chapter 40. Cat

"Nooo! Leave Dr. Lupu alone! Please! I'll tell you everything you want to know. I swear. Please don't harm him. Please!"

"Catherina, you're a cunning woman, and I've wasted enough time playing games with you. Now we'll play my game by my rules." She turned to Ra and Anubis and barked, "Get a move on!" Hurriedly, they carried Tudor to the rack.

I tried to get away from Giselle, but she clamped the back of my neck with renewed vigor. I felt hopeless seeing Tudor with his hands tied behind his back, being placed on the rack and with a harness placed on his ankles.

"I want you to be fully informed of what will happen," said Eleonore. "Impaling is usually performed on the ground. The condemned is placed on his back, his legs spread wide by a harness, and then he's pulled slowly onto the impaling shaft. From what I've witnessed, it is extremely painful. Imagine the stake entering slowly through your ass, up through your intestines, while you're still alive and screaming in agonizing pain. Up between your lungs, and you're still alive and whimpering. If you're lucky, it will not puncture or rip your heart, and you may still be alive as the poker comes out, hopefully, through your mouth. Then the impaling shaft is lifted to a vertical position, and it is planted in the ground so everyone can admire the skewered victim. It is a site to relish." She shivered with excitement.

"What do you want me to do to spare Dr. Lupu?"

"You know, I'm not as cruel as you may think, and there is a chance that I'll spare your beloved doctor. But he will be placed in position for impaling. Rather than being impaled horizontally, Dr. Lupu will be impaled vertically for a more dramatic performance." She motioned with her arm to the two executioners.

I began to cry. Ra and Anubis passed a rope onto a hook on the ceiling, then they tied it to Tudor's wrists and they hoisted him high in the air. The vampires raised the impaling shaft vertically and placed it under Tudor. The harness straddled his legs, and he was ready to be impaled as they attached a rope to the harness and down on the rack around a sheave. Tudor's bottom was suspended one foot over the thick and sharp iron rod.

"Well, he's in position," Eleonore said cheerfully. "As I mentioned, for maximum satisfaction, the whole process needs to be performed slowly. Down there on the rack, there is a mechanism that will pull the rope on the harness very slowly. I would say he might have a minute before the penetration begins."

"What do you want?" I shouted.

"The truth and nothing but the truth. But first, your vampire friends need another jolt." She motioned with her head to Bogdan, who turned the knob.

Angelique, Mundibuto, and François started shaking and convulsing. Spit and drool came out of their mouths, while their eyes rolled up in their sockets.

"More," she ordered.

My friends shook even more violently, and more saliva dripped from their open mouths.

"Stop."

Bogdan, with a stupid sneer on his face, turned the knob back to zero. My friends hung limply on their X-crosses. I couldn't believe it. I'd had my Strigoi pull the lever down. There shouldn't have been any electricity.

And then I realized—the green light was still off. They had faked their convulsions as if they were being electrocuted. Smart.

"Speak!" Eleonore startled me.

"I will." I glanced quickly at Tudor who was coming down slowly. "Upon dying, Vlad asked me to take his ashes and spread them from the tower in Sighisoara during a full moon, which I did. The ashes became a luminescent cloud. Vlady appeared in the tower with Nicolae and Ilie, and took Tudor and me to the crypt under the cemetery, where you kept your army. They placed us in cages suspended over the ground and left us there. I assumed they left to confer with you. Did they call you?"

"Yes, they did, and so far your story is true, except for the black vampire. He was dumped in a hole. Where was he?"

"I don't know what happened to Mundibuto, but he was not with us." I looked at Tudor. He kept descending slowly.

"And then what happened?"

"We were in the dark, and the luminescent cloud from Vlad's ashes came into the crypt. It appeared through the ceiling, and as it descended, it destroyed the zombies and then the proto-vampires. I swear to God, that's what happened. Let Tudor go!"

"You want me to believe that Vlad's ashes had some magical ability and destroyed my army? How were they destroyed?"

"They were burned to ashes, transformed into a coarse sand, something like that. That's what happened."

"Hmm. Then what happened?"

"Vlady, Nicolae, and Ilie came in later, and they went berserk. And then they shriveled and died, disintegrating into sand just like the rest of them."

Eleonore's eyes went wide and she clenched her fists. "I curse Vlad and I hope he burns in hell. That son of a bitch! His goddamn ashes accelerated the aging of all of them." Eleonore paced around, fuming. "Who got you out of the cages?"

"Mundibuto." I looked at Tudor, who was halfway down toward the sharp spike. "That's all there was. I've told you all that happened. Now get Tudor off that thing!"

"And nothing happened to Mundibuto while he was down there with you?"

"No. No. Let Tudor go!"

"Then where in this plot do François and Angelique fit?"

"I don't know. Mundibuto left us. They were not even in Transylvania at that time. Let Tudor go!" I pleaded.

"I guess I'll have to fry the truth out of them after they recover." She glowered at my friends, who were hanging limply from their X-crosses.

"Let Tudor go!" I yelled as loud as I could. "Please!"

She walked back and forth with her hands behind her back. "Dragomir, wake them up." She motioned at my vampire friends.

Dragomir opened up a hose and sprayed my friends with water, and they groggily opened their eyes.

"Listen, you three, and the rest of you vampires!" she shouted. "I'm going to have Catherina Draculesti Sanders sign an abdication document. I want to make sure that there will be no doubt that I'm the only royalty among the vampires. I want all of you to be witnesses to her abdication. Tristan, bring paper and quill plumes."

As any efficient secretary would, he quickly came forward with a small desk, which had papers, writing plumes made of white goose feathers, and a bottle of blue ink. Giselle guided me to the desk and made me kneel in front of it. I resisted, struggled, and got up on my feet. She let me stand. I glared defiantly at Eleonore.

Eleonore came toward me, full of fury. "You goddamn bitch!" She raised her hand to slap me and I tilted my head, not wanting to be slapped on the right cheek; I was still healing from a wound made by a diamond ring in a slap I'd received back in New York. She missed my face, but she slapped me on the side of my head and over my right ear, knocking me to the floor.

I got up on my knees. The pain was beyond description. My right eye began tearing involuntarily. I rubbed it with the back of my hand, but my eye kept on tearing. My ear felt inflamed, and I touched it. I felt something wet behind the ear and when I pulled back my hand, I saw blood.

But soon numbness spread from my ear down my neck. I wiped my eye again and looked at Tudor, who was an inch above the tip of the rod. I crawled to the desk, wiped my tears and my nose with the back of my hand, and said, "What do you want me to write?" I picked up the writing feather and dipped it in the inkwell with a shaking hand.

"Now, that's better. Write, 'I, Catherina Draculesti Sanders, being of sound body and mind, renounce now and forever any claim to the throne of the Vampire Queen Eleonore Elizabeth Amalia Magdalena Von Schwarzenberg.' Sign it and date it.'"

I did as told and rose on my shaky legs. "I wrote what you wanted. Now let Dr. Lupu go."

She took the paper, read it, and smiled. "Very good." She waved the paper for everyone to see. As if that weren't enough, she paraded in front of Angelique, Mundibuto, and François, waving the paper.

"I'd call this an improvement." She looked content with the outcome. "You want me to let Dr. Lupu go when the fun is just about to start? Don't you want to hear Dr. Lupu scream like no man could scream unless he has a poker up his ass?" She glanced at me treacherously. "He must die as payment for what you and your friends here have done to me. You've destroyed my zombies and my proto-vampires, injured my subjects, and killed Vlady and the other two."

"No. You promised."

She came close to me. "Did I? I think not. Instead of impaling him, would you like me to torture him to death? It could last for days. Impaling will take 30 minutes and then he's dead. Besides the screaming and tearing of flesh, it is a humane way to go. Wouldn't you say so?" She looked at me with mocking concern.

Tudor was squirming as he felt the sharp point in his crotch. Ra and Anubis were pulling on the harness rope to keep him in place.

"You are a monster!" I cried. "Go to the hell where I sent Vlady!"

In despair and frustration, I slashed at her with my goose quill plume.

She looked at me with a blank smile, while her eyes unfocused. And then, to my horror, her head fell off her body.

Chapter 41. Cat

I was stunned. Queen Eleonore's body, resembling a headless mannequin, stood in front of me, motionless. I didn't know what to make of what had just happened. My abdication document floated down to the floor from her grasp. Her arms rose and began to flail randomly. The stub of her neck was sliced cleanly, showing blue, coagulated blood were the cut had been made. I looked down and saw her white, beehive-hairdo head at her feet, eyes open wide, staring unfocused.

There was complete silence in the hall. All the vampires were mute with horror and disbelief at what had just happened. The quill, the once white plume, was stained blue now. What did just happen? I didn't know. I didn't have an explanation.

I heard a scream. It was Tudor being impaled.

I raised my hand and broke the shaft in half. "Release him! Now!" I yelled at Ra and Anubis, who did not need a second command and began hoisting him down.

Dragomir was the first to recover from the shock. He howled, "Bogdan, fry them!"

Bogdan went to the panel and turned the knob to the maximum. But nothing happened. The disconnect switch was in the off position, where my Strigoi had moved it earlier. Not hearing any screams or burning sounds, he looked over his shoulder and realized the electricity was off. He moved his hand to raise the lever to the on position, but the entire electrical panel blew outward, as I instructed my Strigoi to do, and Bogdan flew across the room.

Dragomir pulled the queen's sword from its sheathing and leaped toward me, sword raised to cut me in half. Instead, he floated up, spun, and bobbed in the air as if he were a balloon on a string. A moment later, he stopped spinning and flapping his arms, frozen with fear, staring transfigured at me.

I raised the blue-stained feather and twirled it in my fingers. "I beheaded your mighty queen with a feather. Do you want to die for her?" I pushed her standing headless body with the same plume. It toppled over while still squirming.

The sword fell out of his hand, clattering on the floor. While levitating in place, Dragomir pleaded, "No, I don't want to die." He was breathing laboriously. "How did you do that? Your Strigoi have no power against us."

I ignored him and addressed the rest of the queen's vampires. "Let's see how much power I have over all of you." I motioned with my hand and all of them levitated toward the ceiling. Some stood still, while others tried to flap their arms to gain some control over their haphazard, midair positions. They were screaming, groaning, or wailing with despair.

"Release my friends," I requested of my Strigoi. The shackles holding Mundibuto, Angelique, and François burst open. They pushed themselves from the crosses and landed with big smiles on their faces.

"You are our new queen, your majesty," said François, Mundibuto, and Angelique together, all of them dropping to one knee in front of me.

I looked again at the feather, stained with blue vampire blood. My Strigoi must have done all this.

Eleonore stopped squirming. She was finally dead.

I motioned with my hand and lowered the vampires back onto the floor. They slowly approached where the headless queen was lying at my feet, making a semi-circle around her and me. A few even cried, looking at her corpse. Some of them looked at me with fear, some with awe and even respect. None of them knew what to do or what to say. I didn't either.

Angelique was the first to come to my side. She picked up the document that Eleonore had made me write, squished it into a small ball, popped it into her mouth, and swallowed it.

"Get on your knees in front of your new queen!" Angelique shouted at them.

One by one, they dropped to their knees.

"The queen is dead. Long live Catherina Draculesti Sanders, our new queen!" shouted Angelique.

"The queen is dead. Long live, Catherina Draculesti Sanders, our new queen!" all the vampires repeated.

It felt surreal. They were hailing me as their queen. This was madness, stranger than fiction, but I had no time for it at that moment.

I ran to the rack and embraced Tudor, who was in a sitting position with his hands tied. He was in shock and didn't say a word. Anubis cut the rope off his hands.

"Are you hurt, Tudor?" I asked him, caressing his face.

"Cat, you're bleeding." He touched the side of my head and neck. His hand had dried red blood on it.

"It doesn't hurt." I reached behind my ear, and suddenly it dawned on me what had happened.

In her last act of madness, Queen Eleonore had intended to slap me into submission, but because I tilted my head, she instead slapped me on the side of my head, on my right ear. She caused the diamond ampule containing Vlad's vampire blue blood to open, contaminating me.

I was becoming a vampire.

Chapter 42. Cat

I was no longer human. The vampire transformation had begun inside me. That's why I was able to behead Eleonore with a feather. My Strigoi would not harm vampires as long as I was a human, but from the moment the blue vampire blood coursed through my body, I was a vampire, and therefore nothing stopped my Strigoi from harming or even killing vampires. I began to feel their presence, unlike anything I had ever felt before.

I sat down next to Tudor, trying to make sense of the dramatic transformation. In the blink of an eye, my life had changed forever. I began to cry. I was no longer human. I was a vampire.

Tudor kneeled down in front of me and put his arms around me. "What's the matter, Cat?"

I leaned on his chest and bawled. What would become of me now? "Oh, Tudor. It's all over."

"What do you mean? You killed the queen and saved us all. I don't know how you did it, but if you hadn't killed her, I would have been impaled and died in pain. Your friends would have been electrocuted, and you would have been a slave or killed as well. You should be happy."

I looked at him and cried even harder. How could I tell him that I was one of them now? A vampire.

A loud bang came from where the queen's body lay, and the other vampires gathered. Someone had crashed the desk on somebody else's head, and it looked as if a fight was about to start.

It couldn't have been easy for all the vampires to accept peacefully their queen's death. I had to get in the middle of the brewing fight. I got up and ran to them, wiping my tears. "What's the matter?"

Tristan, Trudy, Klara, and Ruxandra were in a small group opposing the others. In between the two groups were Angelique, François, and Mundibuto, trying to keep the opposing groups apart.

"Tristan smashed the desk on Dragomir's head, disagreeing with your right to be our queen," said Angelique.

Tristan glared at me, shaking a finger. "In a moment of confusion, I kneeled in front of you, but now I realize that all this is a sham. You are not our queen!"

"You signed the document abdicating that honor," Ruxandra addressed me angrily.

"Yeah, and where is that document now?" Angelique asked.

"You swallowed it," said a heated Trudy. "That piece of paper is irrelevant. The act of abdication was performed. Right, Tristan?" Trudy looked at Tristan for confirmation.

"And the fact that the abdication was forced on Catherina means nothing?" said Mundibuto. "She signed it under duress."

"Besides, Catherina is from the pure bloodline of Vlad the Impaler," added Dragomir.

"Queen Eleonore is dead," said François. "She brought her own demise upon herself when she disobeyed Vlad's dictum of not interfering in human affairs and spreading vampirism and other mutations. She converted most of you standing here into vampires. And now that she's dead, who would you have as a queen?"

That was a question that they had not considered. What would they do from now on? They were confused, lost.

"But she's not a vampire," said Klara.

"Why don't we sit down and talk about your dilemma. Please," I said. Nearby there was a large, sturdy table with benches around it, and I motioned to them to join me at the table.

They obeyed—some willingly, others reluctantly—and we all sat down. François brought a chair for me to sit at the head of the table. I sat in it somewhat hesitantly.

"You all heard what I told Eleonore about why I came to Transylvania," I began. "It was the truth. I knew that Eleonore and a bunch of you lived here in Transylvania, and I couldn't have cared less. It was not my place to say or do anything about your community and political arrangement.

"Unfortunately for all of you, Eleonore was suspicious of Vlad and of me, and she had me followed by Vlady, Ilie, and Nicolae. Spreading Vlad's ashes in Sighisoara was a simple request, and I obeyed my great-grandfather's wish. I didn't know what his ashes were going to do to the zombie and proto-vampire army, but now that it is destroyed, it is a good thing.

"Your queen would have unleashed Armageddon. In the end, all of you would have been killed. Unless you have a problem with humanity, you'd better reconsider your allegiance to your late queen. Does anyone here have a problem with what I said?"

Many shook their heads.

"Well, I'm glad most of you are in the right frame of mind. As for the subject of who your new queen should be, I didn't wish to be anyone's queen. I didn't come here to claim her throne and overthrow Eleonore. I bluffed that I was claiming the throne, hoping that my friends and I would come out of this alive. Eleonore took my bluff seriously, and these are the consequences." I opened my arms, gesturing around the room where two beheaded vampires lay dead.

"I know that I was declared queen, but I didn't ask for it. Sorry, Angelique, that wasn't my plan. Frankly, I don't care to be your queen. If it's a queen you want—or a king, for that matter—select one from among yourselves."

Loud protestations began among them, some favoring me to be their queen, others not knowing what to do but arguing nevertheless.

I raised my hands to quiet them down. "There is no reason for me to be or not to be your queen. There is no reason for you not to have a monarch of your choice. There is no reason for you to continue under a monarchy, either. We live in modern times. Democracy works. You have choices."

There were no arguments anymore. It might have been a strange notion for them, but they were free to choose, and it was up to them.

"However, I have one warning for you. If you ever consider rebuilding the zombie and proto-vampire army, or making other humans into vampires, I will come back and kill you all." I slammed my fist on the table to make my point clear. The table reverberated from the impact. My vampire strength was growing.

"And how are you going to enforce that as a human?" Tristan asked mockingly.

"First, I want you to know the truth. The luminous cloud did not kill Vlady, Ilie and Nicolae. Mundibuto killed Ilie and I, as a human, killed Vlady and Nicolae."

They gasped at what they heard. Rarely a human can kill a vampire. But here I was a woman who killed two of them.

"Second, I've just become a vampire."

Chapter 43. Cat

I stood up, left them in stony silence, and went back to Tudor.

"Cat, what you told them—is it true?" Tudor asked me with wide, fearful eyes.

I placed my hands on the side of his face and looked at him. "Yes, my sweet Tudor. I've been contaminated with vampire blood, and I'm evolving into a vampire."

"But how? None of them bit you. Was it from the blood spilled when she beheaded Lucian?"

I shook my head. "My great-grandfather gave me a drop of his vampire blue blood, in case I wanted to become a vampire. That ampule was inserted surgically behind my right ear, and it opened when Eleonore slapped me. It was an accident, but a necessary accident for you and my vampire friends and me, so we could live. Except now I'll live forever. As a mutant."

"Oh, my God. I need to give you a transfusion to clean your blood from the pathogen that's infected you. We need to go to a hospital right away." He grasped my hand and pulled me to leave.

"It's too late." I tilted my head and showed him where the ampule was behind my right ear and the dried blood caused by its rupture. "This is the last red blood you or anyone else will ever see from me. My flesh was torn, but now you won't even see a scar. The ampule was probably ejected from my body as well. I heal like a vampire. Look at my right cheek." I touched it. "That's where you treated me for my infection from the diamond ring slap I received back in New York. Do I have a scar? No. My face is smooth, because the vampire blood is taking over."

Tudor touched my cheek and I saw his surprise. "You are cold," he whispered. "Please don't die on me."

"I am cold not because I'm dead but because I'm a vampire. I am very much alive, but a different kind of alive than what you as a doctor would know."

"What will happen to you, to us?" His eyes were full of tears.

"My sweet Tudor. You and I cannot be together. I'm not like you anymore. You have a whole life ahead of you. Find a lovely lady, marry her, and have a family and kids."

He shook his head. "No, I want to stay with you. Make me a vampire."

"You don't know what you're asking. Some vampires wish that they had never become vampires. They would prefer to be mortal again."

"And you? How do you feel about this?" he asked. A tear ran down his face.

"At this moment, I don't know. In the past, I didn't give too much thought about becoming a vampire. I didn't particularly wish to become one, although I was warned that I might not have a choice at some time in the future. Well, the future just happened.

"I thought about opening the ampule and becoming a vampire earlier today in the dungeons. If I had had a clearer head, before Eleonore slapped me, I should have opened it myself to save us all. But I was too tormented, seeing you about to be impaled and my friends about to be electrocuted, and I forgot about the *vampire solution*. Instead, Eleonore did the deed by accident and released the blue blood in me. It had to be done for us to survive."

"But not at the cost of your human nature."

"It is better to be alive than dead. Even alive as a vampire."

"A vampire who lives forever."

"Living forever is overrated. And we will only live forever as long as there is human blood. The life ahead of me will not be paved with rose petals. Vampires will be hunted. Our blue blood could be a weapon, when human armies could be transformed into vampires. And then that will be the end of humanity and vampires alike."

He sighed and looked pleadingly at me.

"Please, forget me and leave," I begged him.

"I can't. I love you."

"I love you, too, Tudor. But it is for the best for us to be apart. Please leave."

We embraced and cried together. His tears felt warm on my cold cheeks.

"Good-bye, Cat. I'll love you until the day I die."

"I as well. And remember, I'm not dead. I'll be around, and you can get in touch with me any time you want." I smiled encouragingly.

We kissed one last time, and Ra escorted him to the garage to leave.

Chapter 44. Cat

Drained and exhausted, I returned to the table. The vampires were waiting for me silently.

"What's the verdict?" I asked casually. I didn't care what they decided to do. I was ready to go back to New York, to my home.

Tristan rose to his feet, followed by the rest of them. "Catherina, your excellence, please be our queen," Tristan said solemnly.

And then they all kneeled.

"What changed your mind?" I asked, surprised.

"Your royal blood," Tristan answered.

"Not to mention that you are the most powerful vampire now," added François.

Yes, that was very true. Before Vlad V died, he was the most powerful vampire, having the Strigoi. Now I was the vampire with the Strigoi, and I was of royal blood. But was I ready to take on such a serious responsibility?

"I'll have to think about this proposal." I saw their disappointed, even desperate, faces, fearing that I might refuse. "Besides, not all the vampires are here at the table. Isolde and Mateo are not here. Also, Ra and Anubis were never part of your conclave. There must be unanimous consensus in order for me to consider becoming your monarch."

They looked at each other, puzzled.

"Dragomir, take Anubis with you and liberate Isolde and Mateo. They must be here as well."

Dragomir left with a short bow, and Anubis led him to the pit.

"Please sit down. I need an answer from you." They sat down and I as well in the chair at the head of the table. "Why are Ra and Anubis so despised?"

Tristan cleared his throat and brushed his hands over his hair. "Ra and Anubis committed treason against Queen Eleonore. They were reduced to the rank of slaves, and the queen transformed them into beasts, what they are today."

"What kind of treason?"

"They wanted to leave the court."

"Why was that a crime?"

"We are her subjects. It's not permitted."

"But all of you, and Ra and Anubis, are free vampires."

Tristan shook his head. "We are your subjects now and must obey you, your majesty."

I sighed. "But François, Angelique, and Mundibuto are free to go as they please."

"They did not swear fealty to Queen Eleonore as we did," said Tristan.

"Let me understand this. If I accept being your queen and you swear fealty to me, you'll be bound to me till death?"

All of them replied affirmatively.

"And you are bound to us, to reign and protect us," replied Tristan.

"Angelique, Mundibuto, François—how do you feel about this?" I asked.

"I have no problem with that," said Mundibuto.

"With all my heart," said Angelique.

"It is the right thing to do," said François. "There are bleak times ahead of us, and it's better to be united. I could not have hoped for a better monarch than you, Cat."

I was stunned. Was this a vampire thing, to obey a monarch? Or, as François said, was it because there would be troubling times in the future?

"I'll have to give some serious thought to this notion."

Dragomir and Anubis returned with Isolde and Mateo. They must have been informed of the new reality at the court, because Isolde and Mateo dropped to their knees in front of me.

"I'm sorry, Isolde and Mateo, for locking you up in the boxes, but it was necessary."

"No need to apologize, your majesty," said Isolde, trembling with fear. Mateo nodded in agreement.

"There will be no punishment for what happened recently. I promise. That applies to all of you."

"Thank you, your majesty," said the vampires, who feared reprisals for what they had done to my friends and me.

"Good."

Ra returned. "Your majesty, Dr. Lupu has left. He asks you if you could give him a call once in a while."

I smiled and nodded.

Ladeena sat quietly at the table, blinded.

"How are your eyes, Ladeena?"

"I don't know, your majesty. I haven't been able to take the bandages off."

"François, can you help her, please?"

"Certainly, your majesty." He walked to her and removed her bandages. "Anyone else who needs vampire medical attention, let me know," he said as he was examining her eyes. "You'll see again, Ladeena. I'll just need to reposition your eyeballs."

Even my friends were addressing me as "your majesty." It made me feel uneasy. I was an American, born and raised in a democracy. This royal stuff needed some adjustments. But I hadn't accepted becoming their queen yet.

François was a good vampire doctor. He readjusted Ladeena's eyes, and she was able to see again. He attended others who were not healing as fast as vampires should, and in a few hours, just about everyone was relatively well and getting better.

We gathered around the table, Ra and Anubis included. I looked each one of them in the eyes, and they were all calm and at ease.

"Earlier, you made me the offer to be your queen, and I told you that I'd think about it," I began my speech. I could see that everyone was waiting with bated breath. "Considering the circumstances we find ourselves in and the fact that I am one of you, a vampire, I've decided to accept the throne and become the queen of vampires."

They all stood up and shouted as one, "Long live Queen Catherina, the queen of vampires!" Then they dropped to their knees and said, "We vampires swear allegiance and fealty to our queen, Queen Catherina. So help us, God."

Yes, even vampires, who are considered the undead but are very much alive, believe in God.

"All rise," I said. "I pronounce you my subjects forever." I thought that was what a newly crowned queen should say, and no one objected. "Please be seated."

I looked around at my court of 16 vampires. "As your queen, I have some new rules. First, Ra and Anubis are reinstated as vampires with equal rights. They are no longer beasts or slaves."

Anubis and Ra stood up, slammed their right fists into their chests, and bowed deeply.

"I will make every effort to undo the transformations of your appearances," I assured them.

They bowed again.

"Does anyone know how their appearances were changed?"

Tristan cleared his throat. "I think I do. There is a special chamber in the cave that may contain the secret."

I nodded and smiled at him. For my own reasons and for my subjects, I was very curious about the ability to transform one's appearance. It could come in useful in the future.

"Next, from now on you may address me as Cat. Let's leave that formal language and 'your majesty' titles for times that will require such formal language at court affairs. I'll let you know when that will be."

They looked at each other, confused.

"I know familiarity breeds contempt, but I am comfortable with who I am and I want us to treat each other on an equal basis. We live in modern times. Even vampires adapt. Any questions?"

There were none.

"If you have questions, you can come and talk to me any time, alone, if you wish. Understood?"

They nodded and I even saw a few smiles.

"And now, if you'll excuse me, I'll need Angelique to come with me to my chamber and help me with my full transition to vampire."

The End

Other Books by Mit Sandru

Thank you for reading my book. If you enjoyed it and would like to help other readers with your comments please write a review on Amazon. And of course I much appreciate your review as well. For more information about my books please visit **sandru.com**
Or visit me at my website: sandru.com and subscribe to my mailing list.
(your e-mail will not be sold or used for spam)

Vampire Thriller & Romance

Vampire (Vlad V, Book 1) by Mit Sandru.
Meeting a vampire isn't something that happens every night, even on the New York City subways. Even in her wildest dreams Cat never expected to meet a vampire or survive an encounter with one. Instead, she becomes his confidant. Why is she so lucky?

R.I.P., The Death of a Vampire (Vlad V, Book 2) by Mit Sandru.

The US intelligence agencies have a massive database, including pictures that can identify any person in the US and abroad. A search has found a photograph of Vlad V Draculesti, a man living in present-day Manhattan, dating from 1851. How can that be? Why does Vlad look the same in the 21st century as he did in the 19th? Who is this man who has lived such a long life?

Homeland Security Federal Agent John Miller discovers that Vlad V Draculesti is a vampire, and he blackmails Vlad for billions of dollars, threatening to divulge that information to the authorities or to the evil Dr. Hellinherr, who is trying to create a super-race of people through the use of vampire blood.

But Vlad V, because of a mishap, is now dying of old age, and all he wants is to die in peace. Cat Sanders, his great-granddaughter, and his three vampire friends—François, Angelique, and Mundibuto—come to his rescue. They foil the intelligence agencies' plans to discover the real identity of Vlad V Draculesti, and they eliminate the corrupt federal agent's threat. Never underestimate a vampire, his cunning great-granddaughter and his vampire friends.

Vampire Slayers (Vlad V, Book 3) by Mit Sandru.

Vlad V the vampire warned Cat that when you're rich, the stakes are much higher, and that she might have to do appalling things to survive. Cat thought she'd have to deal with unscrupulous lawyers, greedy financiers and bankers, Wall Street shysters, corrupt politicians, devious conmen, and depraved socialites. Instead, an old nemesis allied with a vampire-slayer drug cult came out of the dark, demanding extortion money or she would be killed. Capturing a vampire—Vlad V perhaps—would be an added bonus for the cult. Blue vampire blood could provide perpetual life and additional riches. Unfortunately, the villains don't know who or what they are dealing with. Never upset the great-granddaughter of Vlad V and Angelique, her vampire friend, if you want to stay healthy and alive.

Vampires of Transylvania (Vlad V, Book 4)

Cat has a simple task ahead of her: spread Vlad V Draculesti's ashes in Transylvania at midnight during a full moon. But it won't be that simple. She comes across Vlad V and Vlad the Impaler's old enemies and a sinister plot concocted by the Queen of Vampires. By discovering the queen's plot, Cat finds herself in mortal danger.

Luckily, the African vampire Mundibuto and a new friend, Dr. Tudor Lupu, come to her aid. She has to use all the tricks she can muster to stay alive and take revenge on Vlad the Impaler's assassins.

The Queen of Vampires: A New Queen Arises (Vlad V, 5) by Mit Sandru

In Transylvania, Cat Sanders' freedom does not last long. The Vampire Queen, Eleonore von Schwarzenberg, abducts Cat and her friends after they destroyed her zombies and proto-vampires army. The Queen's revenge will be swift, painful, and deadly. Cat and her friends are in grave danger. Will they be able to avoid her wrath and survive?

Science Fiction

Gold Rush Mystery (Terraspantion Chronicles, Bk. 1) by Mit Sandru.

America is back on the Moon. This time, we intend to stay and establish a self-sustaining permanent base for tourism and mining. Our first lunar base is named Gold Rush. Establishing permanent life on our closest, lifeless neighbor is a challenge. But the challenge turns into a mystery when life finds us first.

Time Hole, (Terraspantion Chronicles, Bk. 2) by Mit Sandru. Time Paradox Adventure.

The Moon has many riches, but mining them is a hazardous affair. Deedee and Arno, two lunar generalists, find perils beyond what they signed up for when traveling on the lunar surface at night . . . on the far side of the Moon. Time will not be the same after they fall into the Time Hole.

Folding Reality, by Mit Sandru, a Paranormal, Time Travel Adventure.

Experiencing a new reality is just a paper-fold away for Mike the insurance salesman. But those realities are not by his choice and he ends up being crucified, or gassed at Auschwitz, or marooned in space in a Russian capsule.

Arboregal, the Lorn Tree, by D.G. Sandru, a Teen Fantasy and Science Fiction adventure.

Four young Americans are magically transported to a world where monsters roam the land, magnificent trees support all life, and an evil spirit hunts one of them to fulfill a deadly prophecy.

The Pregnant Pope (TIO Series), by Mit Sandru.

In the year of Satan, 2066, the structure of the physical world is cracking, and inexplicable paranormal forces are interfering with humanity. The Trinity Investigation Organization, or TIO—a paranormal detective society—is the last protection against the demons, evil spirits, fanatical criminals, and sadists who are trying to destroy the world.

The 92-year-old Pope is pregnant. Although he hasn't undergone any medical procedures, he carries a human fetus in his abdomen. Is this a case of self-cloning, or is it a mutation? Is this an immaculate conception, or is it Satan's work?

Claire, Travis, and Prescott, the members of the Capuchin Trinity Team of TIO, are tasked with uncovering the truth about this unusual case and resolving the mystery of whether the Pope is carrying the new Messiah or the Antichrist, and who did it. Their job is to go beyond the physical world into the mind and the spiritual realm, discover a thousand-year-old connection, perform an exorcism, and fight the devil Zepar, while evading the villains who keep trying to assassinate them.

Escape from Communism, by Dumitru Sandru, a True Story and Commentary.

Life under communism is cruel and inhumane. Communist countries have a "Berlin Wall" around them, and the whole country is a giant concentration camp. I risked my life to escape from hell and reach freedom.

T-Shirts and other stuff:

Sandru's Shop or Sandru's Products

Visit my e-Gallery at:
http://dumitru-sandru.artistwebsites.com/
http://www.artistrising.com/galleries/Sandru

About Dumitru "Mit" Sandru

He was born in the greater area of Transylvania in the last century. He is an artist, composer, and author. He paints in the classical, surreal, and modern styles, and most of the music Dumitru composes is of the New Age flavor. As an author, he prefers to write Science-Fiction, Paranormal, and Teen/Children Fantasy novels.

Dumitru resides in California with his wife. They have one daughter and two grandsons.

Visit him at **sandru.com**

www.ingramcontent.com/pod-product-compliance
Lightning Source LLC
Chambersburg PA
CBHW070917180626
46817CB00003B/1096